Quest for Celestia

QUEST FOR CELESTIA

A REIMAGINING OF
THE PILGRIM'S PROGRESS

STEVEN JAMES

Quest for Celestia

Published by Living Ink Books, an imprint of AMG Publishers, Chattanooga, Tennessee (www.LivingInkBooks.com).

Formerly published by Tyndale House Publishers, Carol Stream, Illinois.

Print Edition	ISBN 13: 978-089957-886-6	ISBN 10: 0-89957-886-1
ePUB Edition	ISBN 13: 978-1-61715-267-2	ISBN 10: 1-61715-267-6
Mobi Edition	ISBN 13: 978-1-61715-268-9	ISBN 10: 1-61715-268-4
ePDF Edition	ISBN 13: 978-1-61715-269-6	ISBN 10: 1-61715-269-2

First AMG Printing—March 2012

Cover design by Meyers Design.
Interior design, proofreading, and project management by Adept Content Solutions.

Printed in the United States of America
17 16 15 14 13 12 –B– 7 6 5 4 3 2

To the Barketts

Thanks to Rick for giving this book a new home and to Trinity, Pam, Chris, Liesl, Esther, Todd, and Ariel for your helpful suggestions.

Contents

Prologue

Time is a sea, breaking upon the shore of this moment; and with every splashing wave I remember.

I dream.

A tale unfolds, rising out of the mists. My story overflows before me. Ripple after ripple.

Sometimes when I think of that place and my journey and all the things that happened to me in that land, it all seems so real, so true. Other times, everything seems like a distant dream. The images overlap and blur across each other like a pile of leaves that the wind is slowly blowing away.

I look around and I tell myself that this—this—is real. Here is where I am. Now is when it is. And yet . . . somehow the past gets tangled up with the present. I wonder if time means anything anymore.

Sometimes the scenes from the story seem like only a moment left over from a nightmare, lingering on the edge of my awareness and then simply fading away. Sometimes my dream seems like an entire lifetime. And this is how it began . . .

CHAPTER ONE

The Wizard

I open my eyes. My breathing is fast. Sweat clings to my forehead.

Something happened, I think. *Something bad.*

Shouting in the streets has shaken me awake. Angry shouting. As far as I can tell my parents are still asleep. I decide to see what's going on, to find out for myself. I slip downstairs and into the night.

Packs of frenzied villagers comb the streets. "He's been sighted!" someone yells. "Over by the livery!"

"Find the wizard!" cries a woman nearby. "Protect the children!"

So it is a wizard.

This wasn't the first time a wizard had been sighted in our town. Every few years there would be rumors of someone from the Scaldian Mountains making his way down to our village. The elders claimed the wizards were trying to recruit new apprentices, seduce young maidens, and spread their dark magik. I wasn't sure what to believe. I'd never seen a wizard. But, like all the young men of Abaddon, I was curious.

I decided to see if my friends Erikon and Terrill were awake and would search with me. All of us were sixteen, and I figured that together we could handle a wizard. I slipped along the edge of our house into a side street.

A pale crescent moon ruled over Abaddon that night. Bats skittered along the edge of the light cast by the torches and lanterns. A few faint stars peeked down, but seemed to keep their distance as if they were afraid to come any closer. Though still summer, the air was unseasonably chilly.

I passed another row of houses. Only two more streets and I'd be at Terrill's house.

A few people rode past on horseback, but mostly folks

moved on foot in small clusters carrying pitchforks, scythes, and knives. Most of the faces I glimpsed in the moonlight looked afraid.

I took the shortcut between the blacksmith and the shoemaker's shops. As I neared the alley between the two buildings, I heard a voice: "There you are."

I froze. "Who's there?"

A tall man with a snowy-white beard stepped out of the shadows. I didn't recognize him as one of the men from our village.

"You're Kadin, aren't you?" He spoke with a smooth confidence that was almost hypnotic. "I was sent to find you." He wore a foreign-looking tunic of strange, tightly woven fabric. "You've been chosen."

My heart began hammering inside my chest. I thought of running, but he'd stepped closer, blocking my path. I thought of fighting him, but if he was the one I suspected, that probably wouldn't be a good idea.

"Who are you? What are you talking about?" I tried not to sound too scared, but each word stuck in my throat like a solid object.

He looked briefly to each side to make sure we hadn't been seen. Nearby, on the adjoining streets, I could hear the calls of the armed villagers searching for him.

"Young man, have you heard of the city of Celestia?"

"In tales," I said nervously, "and legends from the ancient days."

"They're not legends. And those days aren't as ancient as they seem." He pulled me toward him then, further into the dark recesses of the narrow alley. The shadows seemed to retreat to give us room to stand. "I'm Alcion."

"Get away from me." I backed up, bumped into a wall. "You're a wizard."

"I doubt that, but call me what you like. The stories of Celestia are true." Urgency threaded through his words. A wild fire burned in his eyes. "Take this." He handed me a brown, leather-bound book, old and worn. On its cover was a drop of crimson.

It was a Book of Blood. A book of sorcery.

I'd heard of them. We all had. My parents and teachers had warned us about these books of sorcery in which every word is written in blood. The elders of Abaddon had long ago banned them, for, as my father told me, they were filled with "dark tales and strong magik."

I stood paralyzed in fear as the wizard slipped the book into my hands. The leather seemed warm, as if it were alive. And it throbbed in my hands like a beating heart.

"No." I dropped the wretched thing into the dusty street. "It's a book of death. I've heard of these. Keep it away from me. Get away from me."

"It's a book of life," he whispered, reaching for the book. But before he could find it, the crowd found us.

Torches flickered at the edge of the alley. "There he is!" A man waved a pitchfork in our direction. "Get him!"

Alcion leaned close and whispered one word: "Soon." Then he backed into the shadows and disappeared into the folds of the night.

I was stunned and breathing fast. I stared down. The book was in my hands again. I couldn't remember picking it up. I'd dropped it once, but now I was holding it again.

The villagers swarmed into the alley, but since I was deep in its shadows, I doubted they could see me. I edged away from them. I could feel the pulse of the book beating between my fingers. A drop of glistening blood dripped from the cover and landed softly next to my boot.

My hands were trembling.

I had met a wizard.

What kind of book is this that bleeds? that breathes?

I threw it down and ran off.

I heard it sigh as it hit the ground.

"Catch him!" screamed the townspeople behind me. "He was with the wizard!"

And with my friends and neighbors chasing me, I ran for my life toward home.

◆ ◆ ◆ ◆

I was quiet the next morning at the breakfast table, but my parents weren't. Talk of the wizard dominated their conversation.

"I heard they almost got him," my father said. "Had him cornered like a rat, but then he cast a spell on them and ran away. Coward. Tried to turn all the people there into snakes."

"Oh, my," whispered my mother. "How terrible."

"I heard he just disappeared into thin air," I offered.

My father shook his head. "No, I tell you, snakes, my boy. Wicked spells. He's a wizard. Conjurer of darkness. Sorcerer!" Then he leaned forward. "I heard they saw someone with him. An apprentice no doubt."

My mother's eyes widened. "An apprentice?"

My father nodded grimly. "A boy. They'll catch him, though. And when they do—"

"Um . . ." I didn't really want to hear what would happen to the young apprentice when they caught him. "What's so wrong with the wizard? After all, what's he done?"

"What's he done? He's a wizard!" he exclaimed, shaking his fork at me. "And don't interrupt me, boy. I'm your father. Now as I was saying, tried to turn 'em into snakes. Started muttering his magik words. I tell you, he came to poison our minds. To poison us all."

"Oh, my," gulped my mother. "Poison us all."

I didn't say anything else. After all, what would have been the point? They could believe what they wanted, but I knew what I'd seen. The wizard hadn't been threatening anyone. He'd been searching for someone.

For me.

After breakfast I headed upstairs to my room. As soon as I opened the door, I froze.

The Book of Blood lay on my bed.

The night before I had left it in the alley. I *knew* I had.

But yet, here it was.

I looked around. It didn't seem like anything else in my room had been disturbed. The window was too small for a person to fit through, and I couldn't think of a way the wizard could have made it into our house to leave it here. The only other explanation—that the book had found its way to my house by itself—was, of course, impossible.

But yet, here it was.

I couldn't stand the thought of being close to the enchanted book so I avoided going into my room all day. But that night when it came time to go to bed, I knew I had to do something.

After gathering my courage, I carefully wrapped the book in one of my shirts, snuck outside and tossed the bundle into the forest. I knew I could never have worn the shirt again anyhow after letting it touch the book. Then I hurried home and crept to my room.

When I arrived, the Book of Blood was on my desk.

During the next few days I left it in a feeding trough, tossed it into the river, and even buried it in a shallow grave near the stables south of town. And each time, it was waiting for me when I returned home. Almost as if it were chasing me. Pursuing me.

What kind of magik is this? I thought.

I considered burning it, but was rather afraid to try. I thought it might find a way to get back at me.

And so at last, after three days of this, I decided to open it up and take a look inside the forbidden book myself. Maybe then it would leave me alone.

I closed the door to my room and locked it. Then, I took a deep breath and picked up the Book of Blood.

My hands were shaking as I flipped open the cover.

Immediately, I recognized the script in the first half of the book. It was the one I understood, the language of our valley, our people. Slowly, I paged through the book, glancing at the delicate script and elaborate illustrations of dragons and caverns and palaces made of light. The pages felt more like skin than paper.

The second half of the book, however, was written in another language. My best guess was that it was Serecean, the language of the hills—Wizard's Tongue, we called it. This section appeared to contain a number of elaborate maps, although without knowing the language, they were meaningless to me.

Once I was familiar with the layout, I turned back to the beginning and began to read.

The content wasn't at all what I expected. The book wasn't filled with dark spells of death or incantations of destruction, but rather with stories and poems of epic adventures. A storyteller had penned this book, not a demented wizard. He told tales of distant kingdoms, giants who lived on the edge of the world, and a prince who would risk all to save his land.

The book also spoke of an ancient evil that had taken up its lair on the edge of the Scaldian Peaks—the very mountains that overlooked our village. As a child I'd heard bedtime tales of such a creature, but this book spoke the story as history, not faery tale. I couldn't understand all of the details, but it seemed to say that the fiend was lying in wait and would one day be unleashed upon our town.

The thought troubled my dreams.

The next morning while I was getting dressed, I glanced into the mirror and saw a black lump resting on the base of my neck just above my left shoulder. In horror I reached up and felt it. The skin was scaly and rough, almost reptilian.

A chill rippled through me.

I felt the lump again.

"The book," I whispered. "The book has done this to me."

The growth appeared to be infected and rooted deeply into my skin.

When I tried to show it to my parents and ask them about it, they looked at me strangely and shook their heads. "There's nothing there," they said.

Even the doctors wouldn't believe me. My mother took me to the finest physician in our town. "Nothing wrong with you, young man," he assured me. "You're just going through a stage. Be patient. Wait it out."

I nodded. "Okay." I didn't tell him that he had one growing out of his neck too. I didn't tell them that they all did. They would have called me mad, perhaps even burned me at the stake as a condemned wizard. There was a pole in the middle of our village for just such a purpose.

Maybe I *was* going mad. Maybe I *was* seeing things.

Or maybe—just maybe—they were all mad and I was the one slowly growing sane.

◆ ◆ ◆ ◆

I knew I couldn't get rid of the Book of Blood—I'd tried that already—but I could stop reading it. So that's what I did. For three weeks I didn't even open it. I kept it closed, hidden under my bed. But during that time, the growth became worse and worse until I could barely stand the pain.

My dreams became darker in those days as well. I was haunted by memories of things I'd done wrong over the years—white lies and cunning plans and forbidden desires—as if reading that book had opened up a gateway in my mind that all the shame of my past was pouring through.

My back, my body, my soul throbbed with more pain each passing day.

You were never meant to live like this. There is another place—there must be another place, another way.

At last I couldn't stand it anymore. If the book had started this torture, maybe it could end it. I opened it up again and read. And the truth is, studying the stories in the Book of Blood did offer some relief from the pain in my neck.

I spent the next couple of weeks poring over the ancient pages, devouring the stories, trying to make sense of them. However, as time went by, the book continued to bleed and my growth continued to grow, becoming more and more painful. I had to be rid of the wretched thing. I had to! But nothing I tried could remove it. Cutting it. Burning it. All of these only made it bleed and scar. Only made *me* bleed and scar.

People began to whisper about me, the young man who'd been seen with a dagger, slicing into his own shoulder and neck, mumbling.

Even my friends Terrill and Erikon began to avoid me. I tried to explain it all to them and to my parents too—leaving out the fact that I'd been reading a Book of Blood—but they wouldn't listen. I told them about the land of the ancient kings and the mystical city of Celestia and how it held out the promise of healing and hope and freedom, but they just laughed. I told them of the ruler of that land, King Kiral, of his wisdom and power and mercy, but they just shook their heads. I warned them about the evil hidden in the hills and the impending danger it posed, but they sneered.

The more time I spent with the book, the stranger and more alive and more desperate and more free the world seemed. It was as if a giant riddle were unfolding before me, drawing me deeper into its heart. With every breath I felt like I was tasting a truer flavor of life.

The book was changing me.

The longer I stayed in the village, the more the book bled. The more my wretched growth ached. And the more I understood I had to leave.

Autumn came, and with it, my seventeenth birthday. Normally I would be considered a man on that day. But instead, I was considered something else entirely. Rumors had taken over Abaddon. Some said I'd become a wizard's apprentice. Others said I'd been cursed, bewitched. I even overheard people talking of the stake in the middle of town.

No one—not even my parents—believed me.

And so, with my birthday came my decision.

The leaves were beginning to turn sickly yellow and drift to the ground that day when I finally told my father I'd decided to leave Abaddon and travel through the mountains to Celestia.

"And how do you know all this? All of these things you keep telling us about Abaddon and this imaginary land?"

I could feel my heart racing. I didn't want to tell him about the Book of Blood, but I realized that at this point I had to.

"I need to show you something."

I led my father upstairs, and he stood impatiently by the door while I crossed the room. The book was under my bed. "Now, when I show you this, I need you to understand—"

"Show me what?"

I took a deep breath, picked up the book and turned to face my father.

His face clouded over with a storm of emotion. Rage. Betrayal. Fear. "Is that . . . ?"

"Yes, but listen it's not filled with—"

"It's the book from the wizard!"

My mother appeared at the doorway and gasped when she saw the Book of Blood.

"He's not a wizard."

"You were reading it?" my mother asked warily. "That's where you got all these strange ideas from?"

I nodded

"It is condemned!" my father roared. "It is prohibited!

"But why? It speaks of—"

"You've been deceived by the magik of that book." A stiff pause. "If you leave, you'll never come back. You'll die up in those peaks."

"I can't stay," I countered. "Either the people will kill me or this infection will. I can't live here anymore. It no longer feels like home."

He looked at me coldly. "That's because it's not," he said at last. "Tomorrow morning I want you out of this house, wizard. Where you go and what you do is up to you."

"Yes," said my mother. "Out of this house, wizard." Then they both walked away

That was the last time my parents ever spoke to me.

◆ ◆ ◆ ◆

That night I wrote them a note telling them how much I loved them. I included directions to the hills in case they ever decided they wanted to leave.

While I was finishing my letter, Erikon and Terrill showed up at my house, and I heard my parents direct them upstairs to my room.

I told my friends about the conversation I'd had with my father, and they listened quietly. Finally Terrill spoke: "Why are you doing this?"

"Doing what?"

He shook his head. "What happened to you, Kadin? We've been friends ever since we were kids, and now all of a sudden you think you're better than us? Our town's not good enough for you anymore? You go around Abaddon telling everyone they've got these infections on their backs—"

"Necks. The infection is on their necks."

"Oh, I'm so sorry, on their *necks.* How could I have gotten that wrong?"

I turned to Erikon. "You believe me, don't you?"

He was quiet. "Is it true you've become a wizard? Downstairs, your father told us you have a Book of Blood."

"I'm not a wizard. It's true that there are wizards, though. Dark forces. Demons and hobgoblins and dragons. The book speaks of them—"

"The book speaks of them," Terrill scoffed. I sensed an uneasiness beneath his words. He eyed the room warily. "I'll bet it does."

"We're worried about you, Kadin," said Erikon.

"Don't worry about me. I'll be okay. You need to worry about yourselves. If the book is right, everyone in this town is in great danger. An evil being will be unleashed."

"An evil being?" Terrill said skeptically.

"Yes. There's a better life out there, in the city of Celestia." I found my gaze landing on the growth on his neck. "You two should come with me."

He just laughed at me. "You're crazy!"

I knew Terrill. There was no changing his mind so I faced Erikon. "What about you? What do you say? Walk with me, just for awhile. We'll travel there together. I'll tell you more about what I've read. There are maps in the book. Maps to a land where no one dies. Where you live forever."

Erikon hesitated for a moment.

"Come with me," I begged him. "My parents won't come. They think I'm crazy. But you believe me, don't you?"

Terrill grabbed Erikon's arm. "Come on. Let's get out of here before people see us talking to this wizard."

"Okay," Erikon said finally, but he was looking at me when he said it. "But just for awhile. Just to see."

"Great." Terrill's tone was taut and harsh. "Now there's two of 'em." Then he pushed past us and trooped out of the room.

I clasped Erikon on the shoulder, making sure I didn't touch the infected area of his neck. "You won't regret it," I said. "I'll see you first thing in the morning."

And so, on the day after my seventeenth birthday, carrying a forbidden book and leading my friend to a land no one believed in to be healed of a disease no one thought we had, I took one last look at Abaddon, and we started on our journey toward the mountains.

The wind tugged at my hair and the words of my father rang in my ears, *"You've been deceived by the magik of that book. If you leave, you'll never come back. You'll die up there in those peaks."*

A voice somewhere deep inside of me told me he was right.

CHAPTER TWO

BAD GROUND

Erikon and I had left Abaddon early, just after sunrise, thinking maybe we could make it to the foothills by nightfall. But as the sun rose high above us and the sweltering day dragged on, we didn't seem to be getting any closer to the mountains.

At first we'd been excited, rushing along the trail, jabbering and laughing as we passed the clusters of sheep and goats that roamed the valley. But as the day wore on, our enthusiasm died, and we plodded along in sweaty, weary silence.

Near the base of the foothills, rivers that started high above us in unseen lands merged, drained through the deep mountain gorges, and emptied into an immense marsh that seemed to grow larger even as we neared it.

The ground became soggier with each step.

Twilight approached.

Erikon groaned. "It's almost like the mud is alive. Like it's tugging at my feet."

"It's just your imagination." I yanked my foot up and plopped it down again on the mucky ground. "Keep going. There's nowhere around here to set up camp, and it's starting to get dark."

"I can see that."

He was right about the ground, though. The earth, solid a few moments before, did seem to be gripping and tugging at us each step of the way. Land became mud. Mud became marsh. And soon, pools of black water swallowed our ankles and rose to our calves.

Erikon stared at the lonely marsh stretching before us. "I've never been this far from Abaddon before."

"Neither have I."

"Are you sure this is the way?"

I wanted to tell him that of course this was the way. Of course I knew where I was going. After all, I had a map right here under my arm, right? I had the book, didn't I? But Erikon seemed more than merely concerned as he glanced at the tangled trees and swampy water surrounding us—he looked frightened. Hoping to reassure him, I said, "Let me check, okay?"

"Okay."

I flipped the book open to the maps. In the dimming light I could see the tangle of squiggly lines and drawings and scribbles, but the maps were all labeled in another language. Before we'd left the village I'd thought I would be able to just compare the maps with our surroundings and figure out which way to go. I hadn't told Erikon that I didn't know the language, that I couldn't decipher this part of the book. I'd simply told him it had maps to the lost city.

The knobby growth on my neck began to itch.

I tried my best to compare the ancient inscriptions with our surroundings, tried to orient the page to the landscape, to figure out which direction to go. But the whole area looked the same, and it was impossible.

"I'm . . . I'm pretty sure this is the way," I said. "We just need to get through this marsh."

Something screeched in the twilight. I told myself it was an owl.

"I'm going back." Erikon's voice was firm. He tugged hard at his leg, but he looked like he was shrinking, getting shorter by the minute. "Something's not right here. And besides, I thought you said you knew the way."

"I do." He was definitely getting shorter. I could see that now. "I mean, I think I do. I'm just not used to using maps is all."

"Not used to using maps," he said coldly.

"That's right."

He shook his head. "Then how are you going to get us to the city, if you're not used to using maps?"

"I'll learn."

"You'll learn."

Yes, he was sinking into the water.

"Um, Erikon—"

The ground had swallowed him up to his knees.

"You're sinking," I said.

"So are you," he said stubbornly, as if that observation alone meant that he'd won our argument. Suddenly, he raised a trembling finger. "What's that, Kadin?"

I heard a gentle slurp a few feet away and saw ripples circling toward us. Something had surfaced and then slipped beneath the water again.

"Okay. Let's go now," Erikon said.

"Right."

But before I could move, the water all around me began to churn and swirl.

Both of us yanked at our legs. Erikon's foot came loose with a squishy jerk, sending him off balance, plopping backward into the foul-smelling water.

In an instant, the water around him became alive.

"Erikon!" I pulled my own legs free and rushed toward him.

As he scrambled to his feet, I saw what was making the swirls in the water. Arms, thinner than human arms could ever be, snaked up from the water and grabbed the cloth of his trousers. Just arms, not bodies. Just arms, growing from the earth itself, or the water. Or maybe something that had died here long ago. Grisly, slender arms, as black as charred wood and each with a clawlike hand.

Erikon saw the arms just as I did. He would have screamed, but stopped himself short. He was staring past me at the water. "Kadin. There!"

Frightened, I spun and looked at the marsh. It had become a sea of grisly arms, black and scaly and wickedly strong. Dozens. Hundreds. Thousands. Curling, twisting, clawing, clutching hands, rising from the water, slicing toward us.

We both took off running, or as near to it as we could, struggling through the thick, knee-deep muck. Sometimes the water became even deeper, and we sank up to our waists. The hands clawed at us and we pulled away and rushed forward. It soon became clear that in our confusion and terror, we weren't heading out of the marsh but further into the heart of it. A mesh of solid branches lurked above us, deepening the twilight with shadows. The day was dying around us in that unholy place.

We stumbled and splashed aimlessly through the water, with the hands chasing us, snatching at us. Trying to pull us back. Trying to pull us down.

Don't fall! my mind screamed. *Don't fall or you'll never get back up!*

My foot caught on a root in the mud at the bottom of the water. I teetered for a moment and then splashed with a dull *thwap* into the soup of hands.

"No!" I cried as I lurched forward.

They were all around me now, tugging me under, grabbing my legs, clenching my hair. I tried to swim, but my face dipped below the surface, and I gulped in a mouthful of the wretched water. The hands, like metal bands, gripped my arms and legs.

I felt something hard slip beneath my armpits, and I knew it was over; I knew I was going to die.

After a quick, desperate breath, my head went under the water one more time, and then in a swirl of pain, everything went black.

◆ ◆ ◆ ◆

"Kadin." A voice was next to my ear. "Kadin, wake up. You're alive. It's okay." Maybe I was dreaming. Maybe I was awake. I couldn't tell.

I had a horrible taste in my mouth, like I'd chewed on rotting meat. I shuddered and rolled to my side, retching, spitting out all I could.

But it didn't get rid of the taste.

"Swallowed some of the water, he did," said a voice that was not Erikon's.

"Will he be okay?" asked the voice that was.

"Depends."

I blinked my eyes open. Obviously we were on a stretch of solid ground. Someone had dragged me here. High above me I could see the moon, round and bold, glowing against the black night. Apparently I'd been unconscious for some time. There was another light. A torch.

We don't have a torch, I thought, slowly coming to my senses. The mysterious voice and the torchlight told me without a doubt that someone else was here.

I sat up. There in the torchlight I could see an old, grizzled man leaning against a long, crooked shepherd's staff. He held the torch in his free hand.

"Almost got ya, they did," he said. His voice was thick and juicy, as if his tongue was too big for his mouth.

Erikon was nodding. "Almost got me too. But we made it, didn't we? Now we can go back home."

The shepherd nodded and tipped his shepherd's crook my way.

I still wasn't quite awake. "Go back home? What?" My arms stung and when I glanced at them, I saw that they bore the scratches of the horrible fingers that had dragged me under the water.

"Home. Yes. Home," Erikon said. "You remember it, don't you? The village we grew up in? On the other side of the valley? Where hands don't suddenly rise out of the water and try to drown you? Home." He shook his head. "I don't know why I ever started following you in the first place."

"To go to Celestia," I reminded him, "and be rid of these horrible growths on our necks. You remember? To be healed. To be free." I twisted my head to look at the bulbous thing that jutted awkwardly from my neck, just above my left shoulder.

In the torchlight it looked the same color as the arms that had appeared in the marsh.

"To be rid of what?" Erikon asked me sharply. "You keep talking about that imaginary growth, that infection of yours, but there's nothing there!"

"Of course there is." I stared at the weird growth just above his left shoulder, deeply rooted to the base of his neck. "And there's one on you too."

He shook his head and grunted softly. "Here we go again."

"Indeed," said the shepherd.

Erikon brushed his hand against the center of the thing on his neck. "See? Nothing."

"Yes, there's—" I began.

"There's nothing there!" he shouted. I couldn't believe it. How could he not see it? Not feel it? He shook his head. "I was willing to put up with you and all of your crazy ideas before, but not now." Erikon motioned toward the swamp. "Not after this. I'm going back. Tonight."

"Indeed," the shepherd said.

Erikon's mind was made up. "If this is what lies on the way, I want nothing of it."

"Indeed," the shepherd said again.

"Would you be quiet?" I snapped. "I'm trying to get him to come with me."

"Oh, you wouldn't want him to do that," the shepherd replied.

Erikon and I both looked at each other and then at the man who had apparently saved us. I directed my question at him: "And why wouldn't I?"

"He doesn't want to go."

Erikon sniffed. "You could say that again."

"Indeed."

"What are you talking about?" I asked the shepherd.

"Oh, it would be much worse for him to go if he doesn't want to."

"See?" Erikon said. "You hear that? It would be much worse for me."

"Indeed."

"Listen—"

"No, you listen," Erikon interrupted. "I'm going back while I still can. And if you were smart, you'd do the same thing."

And then, without another word, he turned and walked into the night. I think he was heading toward our village, but since I had no clear idea where we were, it was hard to tell. The shepherd held the only torch so when Erikon left, he was walking blindly into the marsh.

"Wait!" I yelled, suddenly remembering something I'd read in the book. "It talks about this. The book says there'll be many dangers on the way. This must be one of them."

"Yeah, no kidding," Erikon's voice was already becoming more distant.

"You'll get lost!"

"I'm already lost, thanks to you," he called back. "*Goodbye!*"

And then he was gone.

"Indeed." The shepherd was staring into the darkness that had swallowed my friend.

"Would you stop saying that!" I exclaimed.

Maybe Erikon is right. Maybe you should just go back. You'll never make it through the mountains alone. What were you thinking?

The shepherd glanced at me suspiciously. "A long time, it's been, since anyone has left Abaddon. Half a year, maybe more. Some pass through, o' course." He nodded into the darkness in a different direction than the one Erikon had taken. "But few who are born there ever leave."

I tried to figure out what he was telling me. "Are you saying I should go back too?" I pushed myself to my feet.

"Oh, no." He looked very serious. "Just the opposite."

I looked at him curiously. After a moment when I said nothing, he turned and ambled into the night, skirting along the edge of the marsh, leaving me behind in the darkness. I watched him for a moment, wondering who I should follow—him or Erikon.

The rippling sounds I heard in the nearby water made the decision easy. I hurried after the shepherd.

About thirty or forty paces later I caught up with him. We walked together in silence for a few minutes before I finally spoke up. "What kind of a swamp is this anyway?" There had been terrible strength in those wiry, cadaverous arms. I shuddered to think of what might have happened if the shepherd hadn't reached his curved staff around me and pulled me out.

"Flows down from the hills, it does." He indicated with his staff toward the castle nestled high away from Abaddon. Lights peeked out of the many windows of the high turrets. The stone walls glowed ominously in the moonlight. "Something wicked lives there, something evil. Affects the water."

I blinked. That was where our baron lived; the ruler of our valley. Evil?

The book does say there's a fiend in those hills, perhaps near where the baron lives?

I made note of what the shepherd said but pressed him about the marsh. "But those were hands. *Real* hands. They were pulling me down."

"In these lands, here and in the mountains, good and evil aren't just ideas."

"What do you mean?"

"They're real, my boy. Strong enough to take on flesh and form. Here evil has a face and a heartbeat."

"And hands."

"Yes. And hands. And claws and teeth and scales and fangs and fur. Oh, you have good and evil in your village, but it's veiled. Good is muted; evil is hidden. Like the moon during the day. But here evil shines. Here, it flaunts itself."

"How? Through magik?"

"Oh, no. Something far more powerful than magik lives up in these hills. That's what lets good and evil run free."

His words troubled me. "More powerful than magik? What is it?"

"You'll find out—" he told me, "—if you don't turn back, o' course."

I wasn't really sure I wanted to find out what he was talking about, but if what he said was true—and I couldn't think of any reason why he'd be lying to me—maybe that's why the people of Abaddon were blind to the disease. Maybe that's why the book helped me see the growth I had—it'd come from the hills and was full of whatever lived there that was stronger than magik.

A few steps later, in his torchlight, I saw a hut emerge out of the night.

"Home," he said proudly, although it didn't look like anything to be all that proud of. "Stay here tonight. In the morning, I'll show you where to go to get started." He paused for a moment and then added, "The longer you spend in the hills, the more you'll see. Some of it'll frighten you; some'll comfort you. But out there—" He pointed toward the swamp. "The ground has gone bad."

I'd say so.

We stepped inside the dingy shack, and I slid the pack off my shoulders. I stretched out my neck and rubbed my shoulder around the tender area where the wicked growth had embedded itself. The thing was itching furiously and had started to ache so deeply that my arm was getting numb.

As I began to unroll my blanket the shepherd smiled. "Let me give you a hand."

"No thanks." I gazed out the open window, toward the marsh. "I think I've had enough hands for tonight."

"Indeed." A tiny smile, then he set his torch into a clasp on the wall.

I lay down and tried to go to sleep. But all I could think of was Erikon out there, alone.

Outside, something screeched.

And I knew it wasn't an owl.

CHAPTER THREE

CROSSROADS

The next morning I awoke to the smell of roasting meat, and for a moment it reminded me of the aftertaste of my encounter with the fleshy marsh the night before. I shuddered to even think about that as I rubbed my eyes open.

The shepherd was on the other side of the small hut, bent over the fireplace. Beside him, a stout wooden table held two plates and two mugs, waiting for breakfast. He hadn't noticed yet that I was awake, so I let my eyes wander across the room, taking it all in.

The walls were built of a thick, woven thatchwork made from the sleek branches of the trees that grew in the nearby marsh. The serpentine limbs disappeared into the wall and then reappeared at various places, making it look as if a nest of Baskian vipers had infested the hut and were escaping through the walls when they'd suddenly been frozen in mid-slither.

Other than the table and a cluster of intricately carved walking sticks near the door, the hut was remarkably bare. The shepherd had let me sleep on a mat in the corner of the room, and apparently he'd slept on a blanket that still lay, slightly rumpled, to the right of the table. Considering the sparse nature of his home, I was surprised to see a stack of books on a shelf beside me.

When I saw the spine of the one on top, I caught my breath. It was the same leather-bound style as the Book of Blood in my pack. A quick look at the cover and I could see that the only difference was that his book didn't have a droplet of blood on it, but rather a small white leaf etched onto the leather.

I saw the old shepherd staring at me.

"You have a Book of Blood," I said softly.

"Indeed." He gestured toward the table and set down a bowl of porridge and a plate of roasted lamb chops. "Breakfast."

My family was not rich, and I'd only packed one change of clothes. Last night I'd put on my clean clothes after my original outfit became soaking wet with the wretched water of the marsh. Those were probably still outside in a soggy, reeking heap where I'd dropped them before going to bed. I stood, brushed off my shirt and asked uneasily, "So are you a wizard?"

"Not a wizard, no." He shook his head. "Only a shepherd." He sliced off a forkful of meat.

I sat across from him, my stomach grumbling and my mouth still tasting of swamp water. I drank some of the tea he'd boiled and ate a bite of meat. Everything was delicious. After washing down a few bites of porridge with the tea, I asked him again about the book. "But why does your book have a leaf on it? Mine has a droplet of blood on the cover."

"Oh, that you'll find out soon enough."

We ate in silence for while. Then he asked me why I was heading to Celestia.

"To be healed. And to meet King Kiral himself. I've heard that there, in that land, everyone is free. I read in the book that it is a land like no other."

He stared into space for a moment. "Indeed."

The air blowing through the window felt brisk against my cheek, and the sky outside was bright and invitingly blue. I guessed I could make good time today—perhaps make it halfway to the city. The clear weather and my thoughts of the journey made me forget about the trials from the night before, and I became anxious to be on my way again.

I quickly downed the rest of my meal, thanked the shepherd for his hospitality, then stood. "I suppose I should be going."

Without a word he rose to his feet, reached onto a high shelf, and produced a pile of fabric. "Your clothes."

They were clean, dry, and neatly folded.

I accepted them with my mouth gaping. "But how?"

He gave me no reply but instead stuck his hand into the cluster of walking sticks leaning against the wall. After considering a number of them, he pulled out a staff with intricate engravings along the shaft and the figure of an eagle or a hawk or some type of bird carved into the top. The bird's eyes were inset with emeralds. I had no idea how a poor shepherd could afford such an exquisite staff. To my surprise, he handed it to me. "This will serve you well."

At first I wanted to tell him no, that he'd been kind enough already, that I couldn't accept it, but I could tell by the look in his eye that he wouldn't take no for an answer.

"Thank you," I said graciously, and he gave me a polite nod.

He pointed toward the rolling foothills outside the window. "Follow the trail; stay on the main path. At a pass between two peaks you'll find an inn. You should get there by suppertime, easily enough. Tell the man at the gate that I sent you."

I nodded.

"It's the only way to the city. Be careful who you talk to on the way. And whatever you do, don't arrive after dark."

"Because here evil has teeth?"

"Indeed."

And then before I left, the shepherd handed me a tightly coiled rope that must have been at least a hundred feet long.

"What's this for?"

"It doesn't belong here," he said simply. "You'll know what to do with it when the time comes."

I shoved the rope and my clothes, as well as some food and a wineskin of water that he offered me, into my pack. Then I waved goodbye and started on my way. By the time I found the trail near the edge of the marsh and looked back, he had already headed into the plains to look after his sheep.

◆ ◆ ◆ ◆

For a while the trail meandered along the edge of the marsh. Sometimes short wooden bridges spanned dark tributaries of brackish water. At other times the trail wandered farther into the flatlands of the western plains. The pathway was easy to follow, and it felt good to stretch my legs and find my stride.

Overall, the marsh was quieter and more peaceful here than it had been the night before. Maybe the vile creatures that lurked beneath its waters only awakened at dusk. As I scanned the water, though, I wondered what had happened to Erikon—whether he ever made it back to Abaddon or had gotten trapped in the swamp. I wondered if I would ever see him again.

Even without knowing whether or not he made it to safety, I felt vaguely guilty—as if his choice to turn back had been my fault. I told myself I couldn't have stopped him, that it was his decision, but still, since I was the one who'd urged him to come along in the first place, I felt somehow responsible.

With those thoughts accompanying me, I followed the trail up a small rise and left the swamp behind.

The trail led into the foothills and toward a dense forest that blanketed the lower regions of the mountain range ahead of me. I could see where the rivers flowed down the mountains and emptied into the marsh just as the shepherd had told me. Strong magik of some kind had poisoned that water. Evil magik from high in the hills.

In the forest that sprawled across the base of the foothills were trees of a type I'd never seen before, with deeply grooved bark and huge spreading branches. The trees towered high above me, giving the trail some shelter from the warm sun.

All across the hills the gigantic trees were splashed with the most vivid colors of autumn. From my home in Abaddon, I'd never noticed how distinct all the colors were. Everything seemed to be muted in the village. Here, everything was starkly alive.

The forest both impressed me and intimidated me. Sure, we had small groves of woods in Abaddon, but not sweeping expanses of giant trees like this.

I gazed across the valley one last time.

Abaddon looked small and childish resting there in the middle of the western plains. From here it looked like a hive full of tiny, busy people going about tiny, busy lives. They had no idea that the world spread out expansive and vibrant just beyond the border of their town. Abaddon had been my whole life until just yesterday, and already that world seemed oddly foreign to me. There, life had always seemed so safe and comfortable and important. But now, so much of my time there seemed petty and self-absorbed, and somehow, tragic.

The longer I stared at the village, the more my neck began to itch.

Why didn't I leave earlier? I thought. *Why don't more people venture out?*

Then I realized the morning was passing me by, and I turned and headed deeper into the forest.

◆ ◆ ◆ ◆

High above me, the patchwork of leaves played with the sunlight and threw a tangled web of shadow and light across the ground. The pathway was smooth and gently sloping, and the trail appeared to be well-worn.

Occasionally, I saw other trails merging with the main path, probably from other towns that lay elsewhere in the foothills, hidden from view of my former village. As I was growing up, traders occasionally talked of other towns, but until now, none of that had seemed real or significant in any way.

It was remarkable how big the world had become to me in just a few hours. It reminded me of how, the previous spring, I'd walked past the school I'd attended as a young boy. The building that'd seemed as huge and as wondrous as a castle when I was a child was really just a small two-room enclosure.

The field out front where we'd played endless games of tag was actually rather tiny and closed in. Everything had seemed so expansive and exciting and full of wonder when I was a child.

That's how it seemed to me now. Even the air here seemed richer, fresher, more substantial. I'd lived such a small existence, such a limited life. And now my eyes were slowly being opened—almost as if I were becoming more like a child with every step. Strange. I wasn't sure if I liked the idea or not, but I did like how mysterious and inviting the world was beginning to appear.

I hiked until late afternoon, taking short breaks now and then to refresh myself with a drink or to nibble at the dried meat the shepherd had given me. I wasn't used to exercise, and the path to the inn went steadily uphill, always uphill, toward the mountains.

In late afternoon I came to a crossroads.

One trail veered to the right, and the other ran along the edge of one of the nearby ridges. The ridgeline trail appeared to continue all the way to the baron's castle, which I could vaguely see through the mesh of branches and trees.

I hadn't realized I was that close to it.

Thinking I should check my map, I set the walking stick against a nearby tree. As I was getting ready to shed my pack and pull out the book, the growth on my neck began to itch terribly. When I looked at it, I saw that the diseased flesh was becoming more and more inflamed. When I touched it, pain stabbed deep into my chest.

But it itched so badly I couldn't help but scratch it, even though that made it worse.

I glanced at the walking stick that the shepherd had given me, thought back to awakening in his hut. With a slight chill, I realized something: he had no growth on his neck. Or did he? Had his tunic simply covered it? I couldn't be sure, but I didn't think so.

No, I was almost certain he hadn't had one at all. But how? Everyone in the valley had one. I'd seen them for myself.

As I was considering this, I heard a man call to me from the trail that led to the baron's castle. "Hullo!" he said enthusiastically.

"Greetings," I replied, then repositioned the pack on my back and stepped back onto the path.

Although he was standing in a pool of shadows from the high trees and I couldn't see him clearly, his voice was friendly and welcoming. "And where are you heading, lad, with that load on your back? A long journey, I'd venture to say!" He had something slung across his shoulders, but it didn't look like a pack. I couldn't tell what it was.

He started toward me.

"I'm on my way to the land of the ancient kings."

My words brought him pause and he stood motionless on the path. "You're infected." It wasn't a question.

"How can you can tell?"

"You're coming from the valley." He tilted his head and sniffed at the breeze. "And I can smell it. Can't you?"

I sniffed, but could smell nothing.

"So," he said, "is that part of your journey? To have it removed?"

I nodded. "Yes. And to find Celestia."

He approached me and laughed heartily. Finally I could see what lay across his shoulders—a bow. And on his back he wore a quiver bristling with arrows. This man was an archer. Perhaps he was in the forest today on a hunt. I wondered what kind of game he might be after on this fine autumn afternoon.

My eyes went to his neck; I saw no growth.

"You needn't travel far to be rid of that," he said.

"No?"

"There's a surgeon there at the castle in the employ of Baron Dorjan, Lord of the Valley, who specializes in removing those tumors. And as for journeying to Celestia, I'd advise against it." He was only a few paces away, and as he stepped closer he lowered his voice. "There are dangers in the high hills that you would do best to avoid."

"Yes. The shepherd warned me of those."

"The shepherd." I couldn't read his tone.

"That's right. Tell me about the dangers."

"Ancient creatures. Things of legend that take the form of serpents and winged beasts from another time. Gryphons and dragons and giants and thieves. Wolves roam those hills. Fierce and untamed. Some people say that evil itself lives up there and can take on any form it desires. Some claim to have seen ghouls prowling in the mists and heard them whispering thoughts into their heads."

A chill snaked down my spine. "Strong magik. Evil with fangs."

"I've never heard it put that way, but yes." He gestured toward the baron's castle. "But there's another way."

"I thought there was only one way to Celestia? I was told this is the only path."

"Yes, of course, only one way to Celestia, but there are many ways to many places just as good. If you can have all that Celestia offers, all that your book—you do have a book?"

"How did you know?" His knowledge of me was amazing.

"Experience." He nodded toward my pack. "If you could have all that your book promises you, but without the dark journey, wouldn't you accept that?"

"Perhaps," I said cautiously.

He swept his hands out, palms up. "The baron can give you everything you've been hoping for without any of the pain of a trip through the mountains." He gazed past me at the trail leading away from the castle. "Son, there's no road more dangerous than the one you've chosen. Why anyone would ever take it, I never could understand."

I remained unconvinced, and I think he could tell. He put

his hand on my shoulder then, and sliding it to the growth on my neck, he began to pick at the swollen sores. I winced and backed away.

"When did you first notice this?" he asked.

"When I read the book."

"Precisely, my friend. Don't you see?"

I eyed him. "See what?"

He sighed softly. "Of course not. You don't see. How could you? You've been deceived by a wizard. No, you don't understand anything. That growth is the result of his spells."

"I don't believe you."

"No? Did anyone else in Abaddon read this Book of Blood?"

I shook my head.

"And no one else saw any kind of growth on themselves or on you, I suppose?"

I paused a moment before answering, the impact of his words slowly sinking in. "No. They didn't."

"So, you read a wizard's book and started seeing things, started feeling a cursed growth on your neck that no one else noticed." I wasn't sure if it was a question or simply his conclusion.

"But you just picked at it," I noted. The sun was slipping behind one of the mountains and with each passing moment the shadows of the tall trees were growing deeper.

"I've met others who were cursed as well. The wizard's spell still lingers over you. Can't you see how he's using it to lure you into the hills to your death? Come with me, and we'll have this all straightened out by suppertime." He started back up the trail toward the castle.

I watched him leave. Did not follow.

The archer called over his shoulder to me, "It'll be dark soon. Believe me, you don't want to be out here in these woods at night."

That's the same thing the shepherd told you.

I was still hesitant to go with him. He'd mentioned a surgeon who could remove the tumor and then implied that I was only seeing things.

But I had to admit that on one level, some of what he'd said did make sense. Wherever this inn was, I doubted I would still be able to make it by suppertime. If nothing else, I could spend the night at the baron's castle—keeping a careful eye out for danger—then continue on my way in the morning.

And, it was possible, of course, that I *had* been bewitched.

In the end, the prospect of receiving all of the benefits of Celestia, everything I sought, without any of the dangers of a trip through an evil land was just too tempting.

"Okay." I turned toward my walking stick. "I'm coming."

CHAPTER FOUR

DOGS

The staff was still leaning against the tree only a few feet away. I reached for it, but my hand glanced across the carved head of the bird, and the walking stick slid away from me. Before I could grab it, the walking stick bounced and tumbled downhill about twenty paces from where I stood.

"I'll be there in a minute," I called to the archer. "My staff fell down the hill. I'll be with you as soon as I get it."

"Forget it," he laughed. "We'll get you a new one."

I thought back to the shepherd and how he'd helped me, given that staff to me. "No. I'll be right back."

For a moment I considered taking off my pack while I scurried down the hill to grab the walking stick, but that would slow me down, and my guide seemed to be in a hurry. Instead, I stepped off the trail with my pack still on and, using one tree after another for support, maneuvered my way down, descending into the ravine. It was awkward and slow, but I told myself that with the walking stick, getting back to the trail would be easier than picking my way down the hill.

The staff lay next to a downed tree; a wild thicket had grown up around its thick network of branches. If the stick had landed in there, I might never have found it.

As I leaned over to pick it up, a voice whispered to me from the middle of the thicket: "Don't go back."

Startled, I jerked my hand back. "Who is it? Who's there?" I studied the underbrush but could see no one.

"Don't go with him." The same voice. Urgent and pleading and loud enough for only me to hear. A girl's voice.

"Who are you?"

"Be quiet and listen. He's not a friend of the shepherd—"

"The shepherd? You know the shepherd? Who are—"

"—You're talking again. I said *listen.* You don't understand anything do you? The archer works for the baron." Still I couldn't see who was talking to me.

"Yes, the baron," I said. "He's going to help—"

Just then, the archer called from the path, interrupting us: "Are you okay down there?" His voice didn't sound nearly as friendly as it had a few moments ago.

In the distance I heard the sound of dogs yelping.

As I stared at the thicket, a face slowly materialized on the other side of the tangled branches. The face of a young woman. "Come with me. We don't have much time."

"Why? Who are you? Why should—?"

"You ask too many questions. Let's go."

The warnings of the wizard rang in my ears: *"Be careful who you talk to on the way."* I knew from reading the book that there were people in these woods who would try to deceive travelers, to lead them astray.

The archer?

Or her?

I still couldn't make out her features, only the outline of her face. But I knew one thing—she was definitely not encouraging me to stay on the path.

The voice of the archer came from the trail. Icy and cold. "Kadin, are you coming?"

"He knows my name?" I said to myself. "But I never told him my—"

"Of course he knows your name," the girl said, then slid her hand out of the underbrush. "Come on."

At last I saw the face of my would-be rescuer. She looked about my age, old enough to marry but not yet in her second decade of life. Dark, tangled hair framed her face. Her startling hazel eyes were piercing and intelligent but filled with something that looked like either confusion or terror. I might have described the rest of her face as attractive, even lovely, if it hadn't been covered with horrible bruises. Someone had beaten her.

"What happened to you?" I asked.

The rustle of leaves above me. The archer was coming. "Kaaaadin!"

"Come or stay here," the girl hissed. "It's up to you. I'm leaving." And then, in a whisper of movement, the face was gone.

The archer?

The girl?

"Hey, wait for me," I called, but it was too late. The fading sound of crunching leaves told me she'd already left. I was amazed that she could move at all through underbrush that thick, let alone scurry away so swiftly.

The distant braying of wolfhounds had turned into excited howls now. They were closer. Onto someone's scent.

"I can smell it," the archer had told me. *"Can't you?"*

Oh no.

The infection.

Above me, the sound of breaking branches—the archer had left the trail and was descending the ravine. In a chilling moment I realized what kind of game he was after.

Grabbing my walking stick, I ducked below a couple of branches and ran into the forest. Stiff twigs snapped against my face and forearms, stinging me, but I kept going.

"Kaaaadin, the baron wants to meet you." He was mocking me now. His voice carried no doubt that he would catch me. I wondered how many other travelers he'd been sent to track down in this forest.

My foot slipped; I tumbled for a moment, then righted myself and started to run.

Trees flashed past me as I bolted through the forest. The sun had dipped past the mountains, and the chilled shadows of nighttime were taking over. The world that had seemed so broad and beautiful to me earlier in the day began to feel wicked and threatening.

You should never have left the trail. You should never have talked to that man!

The forest thinned, and I saw another ravine just in front of me. One moment too late I tried to skid to a stop, but I was going too fast and toppled forward. Everything became a blur as my body bounced and tumbled down the ravine. I was vaguely aware of the sound of the dogs above me, or beside me, or below me, I couldn't tell—maybe I would land right in their midst. A sharp pain in my ankle told me I'd done more than just plummet over the edge—I'd sprained or broken something in the process.

I held one arm up to protect my face the best I could, and with the other I somehow managed to hold on to the walking stick. The forest whirled past me until, finally, I came rolling to a stop at the base of a great tree covered with tendrils of dried moss.

Rising unsteadily to my feet, I shook the leaves from my clothes. Pain from my ankle shot up my leg. During my descent, the left shoulder strap to my pack had ripped loose, but miraculously the other strap had held. Night was crawling into this ravine, but the crimson sky still held enough light for me to see a path cutting through the underbrush about thirty paces in front of me. I hobbled toward it and then froze as an arrow sliced through the twilight and struck a tree less than a foot from my face.

I whipped around, dropping to my knees.

The archer stood on the ridge of the ravine. "You should have come with me, Kadin. Now we'll have to do this the hard way."

As he raised his bow, I ducked behind a tree.

Swish. Another arrow sailed past me. Then another. I crouched and half crawled, half scurried toward a larger tree. I peered back at him through the forest, trying to catch my breath. Thankfully, the archer was still some distance away, but it looked like he had found a switchback trail and was coming closer. He'd nearly hit me all the way from the ridge; I hated to think how accurate he would be if he were any closer. My tumble down the second ravine might have actually helped by putting some distance between us.

Ahead of me, maybe two hundred paces or so, I could just make out a wall nestled against the sky.

The inn.

A narrow trail curved toward it, but steep cliffs dropped precariously to either side. Once I started on that trail, there would be no turning back and no place to hide.

But according to the shepherd, the only way to the mountains was through that inn. I had to make it.

I ventured a quick look back toward the archer. Three wolfhounds were rushing past him, growling and bounding down the hill straight toward me.

Go!

Pushing myself to my feet, I rushed as fast as my ankle would allow me toward the inn, branches snatching at my clothes as I did. The pain in my leg exploded with every step, but I tried not to think about it—it seemed like a small thing compared to an arrow in my back or a wolfhound at my throat.

I was on the trail to the inn. Running. Pounding. I could smell the smoke of their cooking fires.

The inn rested on a steep mountain pass dimly visible in the settling darkness. The dogs burst out of the trees less than fifty paces behind me.

But it was almost that far to the inn's door, which stood in the middle of a wall between two lookout towers.

Apparently the sound of the dogs had awakened someone inside the inn because by the time I was within earshot of the door he called to me, "Who are you?"

"Kadin," I hollered without thinking—of course he would have no idea who Kadin was. "The shepherd sent me!"

A pause. "He never sends people at night."

"Wrong path," I yelled, half-out of breath. "Please!"

The dogs barking, closing the gap between us.

Ten paces to the door.

I could imagine getting all the way there and then becoming cornered by the dogs or pinned down by the archer.

Open it in time!

Please open it in time!

As I arrived, an arrow kicked up a cloud of dirt near my left foot. I grabbed the handle of the enormous door and yanked. Locked. I tried banging my weight against it. Nothing.

"Please!" I called to whoever might be on the other side.

I turned back just in time to see one of the wolfhounds leap at my face. I swung the walking stick hard, catching the dog in mid-air. With a sickening crunch, the dense wood connected with the side of the beast's head, sending the dog sprawling onto the ground while the other two bounded toward me.

I jabbed at the two beasts while they snapped at me, baring their teeth.

"Hurry!" I cried to the man behind the door.

"The bolt is jammed!"

"Unjam it!"

The dog who'd come at me first was on his feet again, coming at me. I kicked at him, well aware that his jaws were big enough to bite through the leather, through the skin, through the bone, but hoping he wouldn't be able to get the right angle. Thankfully—

"Back!" I swept the walking stick in front of me again to clear the dogs away and heard the *thunk* of another arrow. I gasped, knowing it had struck my chest, that my journey was over already. But I couldn't find an arrow sticking out of my body anywhere.

Then I saw: it had struck the walking stick, embedded itself into the wood between my hands.

Behind me the bolt disengaged, and the heavy door swung open.

I spun on my heels and jumped through the narrow opening as the dogs lunged toward me. Two more arrows sailed past my face and stuck into the oak door as I ducked inside.

The man on the inside slammed the door shut, almost taking off the head of one of the wolfhounds.

Struggling to catch my breath, I collapsed onto the ground while the guardian of the door pushed the bolt shut. He peered at me as the dogs threw their bodies against the door behind him, the force of the impact shaking the entire wall. "We do not typically open this door past dusk," he told me severely.

"I can see why," I replied, still gasping for breath.

I struggled to my feet, felt my ankle give way, and I would have fallen had I not caught myself by grabbing the arm of the man beside me.

"I'm Kadin," I told him.

"Yes, so you said. My name is Tobal. I'm the doorkeeper."

"Thank you, Tobal," I was finally catching my breath, "for opening it in time."

Outside I could hear the archer cursing and calling out threats against both me and the doorkeeper. The dogs were still barking and clawing at the door.

My pack was hanging awkwardly by its one good strap, my face and arms were laced with wicked cuts from the branches, my ankle was tender and painful, and my clothes were muddy and tattered from my fall into the ravine. Bloody and bruised, I just stood there breathing heavily, trying to smile at Tobal, as I leaned against his arm for balance.

He assessed me. "You look like that and you haven't even started your journey yet?" He shook his head, then picked up my walking stick and handed it to me. "Watch out for that arrowhead; they're usually poisoned."

I stared at the arrow. "What do you mean I haven't even started my journey yet?" Leaving me to balance my weight on my staff, the doorkeeper walked away. "Tobal?"

I didn't want to touch the poisoned arrowhead, so I left it embedded in the walking stick, but I snapped off the shaft of the arrow, tossed it to the side, and hobbled after him.

"Excuse me," I called again. "What do you mean I haven't even started yet?"

CHAPTER FIVE

Dreams

Limping, I followed my host down a hallway lit by torches set in elaborate holders every five or six feet. Halfway down the hall, a large dining room with a roaring fireplace opened to the left.

The entire inn, except for the stone fireplaces, appeared to be constructed of heavy beams and massive logs, presumably harvested from the towering forests of the surrounding hills. The place was built more like a fortress than anything else. And judging by what I'd seen so far of how friendly the neighbors were, that was probably a good thing.

Seated at one of the tables in the dining area was the bedraggled girl I'd seen in the thicket. Apparently she'd found her way here before me. Maybe she hadn't taken the vertical detour through that second ravine like I had.

The moment she saw me, she shook her head and looked away.

I hadn't noticed before that I knew her, but now in the light of the inn, I recognized her. She'd grown up with me in Abaddon. We'd played together as children. Over the years we'd lost touch with each other, but about eight or nine months ago I'd heard she'd disappeared. Some people said she'd been killed or kidnapped by bandits. Others said she'd gone to work for the baron. As the ruler of our valley, he often invited women from Abaddon to join him at his castle. No one really questioned it when he called for them. I couldn't recall exactly what kinds of jobs my father had told me he offered to the young ladies he summoned, but now that I thought about it, I remembered that he seemed to like his helpers young and unmarried.

"You're from Abaddon, aren't you?" I took a seat across the table from her.

A cloud of emotions crossed her face. "A long time ago, yes, I lived in Abaddon."

Eight months didn't seem all that long to me. But after another look at her bruised face it struck me that eight months could be a very long time indeed.

"You're Leira, aren't you?" I said. "I'm Kadin." I extended my hand to her. She didn't take it.

"Kadin?" She seemed to be searching her memory.

When she didn't shake my hand, I drew it back. "Yes. We played together in the yard in front of the school. When we were children." So, I'd found the missing girl after all. I smiled. "It's you. It's really you."

She scoffed, took a small bite of food. Swallowed. "I try to save your life, and in return you lead that archer and those dogs right up to where I'm hiding, and now what? Maybe you want to run off and play tag again? I barely made it here in one piece. A small 'Thank you' or 'I'm sorry' might be in order."

"I didn't know you were trying to save my life. I thought maybe you were one of them."

"Then why would I be hiding in a thicket?"

That was not a bad point.

"How was I supposed to know who you were? I didn't need you to save my life."

"Is that why those wolfhounds are still chewing away at the door as we speak?"

"Well, maybe they were after you, not me."

She looked at me long and hard, her eyes turning colder and more distant each second. "Just promise me that you'll stay out of my way from now on."

"Fine."

"Okay."

"All right then."

"Good." She stood and headed to the fireplace where she turned her back to me.

Nearby, Tobal was bringing me a plate of food. "That went well," he said to me as he set down the plate. "Not only are you an expert outdoorsman, I can see you're also a real charmer with the ladies."

I just stared at him.

"Enjoy your meal," he said wryly, then glanced at my tattered clothes and injured ankle. "Try not to hurt yourself with the silverware."

I watched him walk away. "Oh, that's very funny," I muttered. " 'Try not to hurt yourself with the silverware.' You oughtta be a court jester somewhere."

So far my trip had been nothing like I'd expected—a deadly marsh, archers, dogs, and now a sarcastic doorkeeper. Sure, I'd known things would be tough at times, but not like this. And if Tobal was right, my journey was just getting started.

Halfway through the meal, I looked up from my plate and saw a distinguished-looking woman with gray-flecked hair striding down the steps. She smiled at the servants, and, when she reached the bottom, whispered a few words to Tobal who in turn nodded and began hobbling around acting like his ankle was hurt. Then he pointed at me.

Oh, great.

The woman, whom I took to be the owner of the inn, approached me. Her eyes narrowed in such a way that I couldn't tell if she was being inquisitive or judgmental. "So you're the boy from the village who came knocking after dark."

I didn't especially like being called a "boy," but nodded. "Yes. Kadin. Sorry I arrived so late in the day."

"Reyhan," she said with a short bow. "I'm the keeper of this inn."

Her eyes traced the outline of my face and landed on the growth on the side of my neck, but they didn't linger there for long. "And why have you come alone, Kadin?"

"The people in my town accused me of being a wizard's apprentice. They wouldn't come with me. My friend Erikon started the trip with me, but when we got to the marsh, he turned back for home."

There was a deep sadness in Reyhan's eyes. "I see."

Leira turned our way, and Reyhan joined her by the fireplace. After a moment she gently touched the bruises on Leira's cheek.

I expected her to flinch but she didn't.

"You," Reyhan said, "are a very brave and a very foolish young woman." Leira looked down as if she were ashamed of something, but I couldn't figure out what that might be. Reyhan lowered her hand. "The baron did this to you." It might have been a question, but she said it in a way that showed she already knew the answer.

A single tear began to course down Leira's cheek. The tear glistened in the firelight, clung to her jaw for a moment, and then dropped to the floor. I could only wonder what kind of nightmare she'd lived through at the hands of the baron. I'd always heard that he was kind and gracious—and I'd believed it. Not anymore.

He didn't release her, I thought. *She escaped.*

Reyhan looked in my direction again and gave me a curiously mischievous look. "Well, you two have quite a journey ahead of you."

"We're not traveling together," Leira said bluntly.

Reyhan feigned a look of surprise. "You're not? Oh. I see. Well then, it'll be an even harder trip than I thought."

And with those words, Reyhan the innkeeper left for the kitchen.

◆ ◆ ◆ ◆

While I finished eating, Tobal led Leira out of the dining area, presumably to her room. A few minutes later he reappeared beside me. "If it doesn't sound too dangerous, I'd like to take you to your room."

"Do you get paid to give your guests a hard time," I grumbled. "Or is it just a hobby?"

"Up until now it's been a hobby, but maybe I should make a career out of it. What do you think?"

"I don't think you'll have any trouble landing a job."

He smiled. "Come on. Follow me."

Despite his sarcasm, I was beginning to like this man. He looked about ten years older than me, and like everyone else I'd met on my trip so far—except for Leira—he had no growth on his neck. Just a small scar in its place. His face was carved with sharp, elegant, almost regal features. His long dark hair had been pulled back into a thick ponytail that swished across his shoulders when he walked. Tobal moved with an air of sophistication that made me think of royalty, but he'd also shown great strength and speed slamming that enormous door shut to keep out the dogs. I wondered what life Tobal might have left behind to come here and work as a doorkeeper.

After we'd ascended several flights of stairs and arrived at my room, he set down my pack, which he'd refused to let me carry when he saw the severity of my limp. Before bidding me goodnight, he patted me on the shoulder that was not infected. "Kadin, you'll find that in these hills your heart often awakens when your body sleeps. Pay special attention to your dreams tonight. This land is different from the one you grew up in. There's something here that's even stronger than magik."

"That's what the shepherd told me. Almost the exact same words. So what is it? What's stronger?"

He removed his hand. "You'll find out."

"Are you sure you can't—"

"You'll find out."

"Right," I mumbled. "The shepherd said that too."

"Breakfast will be served at eight o' clock sharp. Don't be late."

"I won't."

Tobal turned to leave, then stopped. "One more thing. You may want to sleep on the floor instead of the bed tonight."

"Why's that?" I said nervously. "Magik?"

"No." A smile creased his face. "So you don't fall out of bed and hurt yourself."

"Very funny."

"Good night."

"Good night, Tobal."

He shut the door, and I was alone in the room.

It was sparsely decorated but inviting enough, with a bed in the corner, a writing desk with a lantern, and double doors that led to a small balcony overlooking the valley. Beside the bed was a nightstand. The room was heated by a small fire burning in a fireplace set into the wall.

I placed my things beside the desk and pulled out the Book of Blood. The blood on its cover was still fresh. Moist. I placed the book on the nightstand, then pressed open the door to the balcony and stepped outside. The stars gleamed far brighter than I remembered them ever glowing above Abaddon. And they seemed oddly close here, almost within reach.

As I scanned the horizon, I noticed the baron's castle on the next hill over, and in the distant torchlight, the outline of archers poised on its tall towers. I assumed I was out of range, but they still made me uneasy.

Somewhere close by I could hear crickets chirping and, in the distance, the howling of wolfhounds. My room was above the tops of the trees, giving me an unobstructed view of the valley. Far below, a pool of lights revealed Abaddon's location.

I heard something else coming from the next balcony over. Soft whimpering sounds. I eased closer. Leira was there, sitting in the starlight with her knees drawn up to her chest, her hands against her face, crying.

"Leira?"

No reply.

I walked as close to her as my balcony allowed. "Leira, are you okay?"

A pause, and then through her tears: "I'm fine. Leave me alone."

A moment passed. I tried to think of how to help.

"Hey, I'm really sorry for what I said earlier. You did help me. If you hadn't showed up I'd probably be dead or in chains."

I heard her exhale sharply in agreement.

"Leira, thank you."

Silence that grew more and more awkward.

"Okay. Goodnight, then." I turned to go back inside.

"Wait." She sniffled softly and then looked my way, wiping at her face.

The starlight danced in her matted hair. A soft glow enveloped her, making her look for a moment more like a faery or an angel than a haunted and abused young woman.

"I'm glad you made it past the dogs," she said at last. Then without another word she turned and headed into her room.

Well, it was a start.

I stayed on the balcony for a while watching the sky, hoping to see a shooting star. When none appeared, I went back inside and crawled into bed, weary, confused, and dead-tired, wondering how many nights Leira had cried by herself in the dark over the last eight months.

I'd barely flopped my head onto the pillow before I fell asleep and began to dream.

◆ ◆ ◆ ◆

I dreamt that I was walking along a trail in the forest when I came to a mist-covered meadow. All around it, tall thickets of wild vines and wicked thorns grew unchecked, but in the clearing itself there were only flowers and, at the crest of a hill in the middle of the meadow, one tall tree. The thorns seemed to lurk and writhe on the edge of the mist like barbed serpents. But they could not enter the field of flowers.

The single wide-branched tree was willowy and fair. Its leaves rustled slightly in the breeze, more like feathers than anything else. Mists curled through the day, and the diffused glow of sunlight warmed everything. A few leaves dropped from the tree as I approached, as if the branches had let go of them to welcome me. The leaves curled on tufts of air, twisting and rising gracefully around me, then settled softly onto the ground by my feet. Everything in my dream moved at a slower, more deliberate speed than things do in the waking world.

On the edge of the hill beneath the branches of the tree, the mouth of a dark cave gaped open. Deep hissing sounds rose from the cave as if maybe it was the home of a great serpent or dragon. I wanted to avoid the cave but found myself fascinated. Both repelled and attracted by the scene, I stepped closer.

Once under the tree, I touched some of the leaves still on the branches. They were as light as air and tickled across my palm like a mother might touch the hand of her child, like a young groom might caress the cheek of his bride. Only then did I see what oozed from the bark of this tree.

Blood.

I stumbled backward and spun to get away but felt something tuck beneath my arm and curl around my chest. My hands flew up to protect myself, but the branch held me fast. The tree was reaching out for me. Pulling me in.

"No!" I tried to wrestle free.

And where time had been slow before, now it seemed to rush forward. In a swirl of movement, another branch curled around my legs and a third around my right arm. The grip was impossible to break. Then the tree in my dream was lifting me. I struggled, but it was no use. The branches were iron fetters wrapped around me.

A rush of terror.

Thoughts as dark as night swirled through my mind. Memories of lies I'd told, insults I'd given, arguments I'd started, friendships I'd ended, apologies I'd left unsaid, selfish motives I'd had. All of my failures and misdeeds swarmed through my mind as the branches wrapped tighter and tighter. The enchanted tree was haunting me with my past just as my nightmares had done in Abaddon when I first read the Book of Blood.

I knew the tree would rip me apart, or throw me into the writhing thistles, or perhaps feed me to the hissing cave. It would end here. Everything would end here.

But as the tree lifted me into the heart of its branches, I didn't feel any pain. The feathery leaves touched gracefully against me and, as strange as it sounds, I thought I heard music—like the soft melody of the wind passing through the forest. Each leaf seemed to become another note in the song, and together they formed a perfect harmony, both primal and new, that enveloped everything.

The tree lifted me high above the meadow, and all I could see were the white feathery leaves passing before me in the misty air. The branches brushed against my back, against my shoulders, as if they were caressing me. Slowly then, and gently, the tree set me down on the hillside. As the branches retreated, I could see more blood oozing from the bark of this strange tree, pooling on the ground and staining the white leaves that had fallen to the ground.

I sat there on the hillside staring at the mystical tree, unsure what to do or what to think. And that's when I saw that it held something else in its branches, something black and smoldering. A dark lumpy thing with tendril-like roots, wriggling to be free.

The tree seemed to groan, and then with a sharp crack that echoed across the meadow, the branch holding the wretched mass broke off and fell into the cave as if it had been chopped off by an invisible axe. I heard a sharp and ear-splitting screech; then the thing was gone and the hissing in the cave ceased.

A breeze carrying the fragrance of lilies glanced across my face. I stared at the tree. In the place where the great branch had broken off, dark drops of blood fell to the ground.

Then I watched my hand rise to my neck and as I felt for it, I found that the growth was gone. The infectious tumor had been removed. In its place all I could feel was a small, gently curving scar.

And that's when I awoke.

◆ ◆ ◆ ◆

The night was still. Crickets still jabbered from somewhere in the shadows outside the window. Elsewhere in the inn, the workers and other guests must have all gone to sleep, because there were no other sounds except for the occasional scurrying of a mouse somewhere in the walls.

I brushed my hand across my forehead and found it dripping with sweat.

My breathing was heavy, and I tried to calm myself.

A dream.

It was all a dream.

This is reality.

I looked around the room for something—anything—abnormal. The dream had seemed so dangerous and terrible and glorious and real that I expected the whole world to have changed. But everything appeared to be just as I'd left it.

Still, I felt uneasy. Favoring my ankle, I retrieved an ember from the fireplace, lit the lantern on the desk, and trimmed the wick. Soothing light eased into the room.

I gasped.

The Book of Blood lay on the nightstand right where I'd left it, but on its cover the drop of moist blood was gone. In its place was a soft, white leaf.

I brushed my hand against it to see if it was real or if maybe I was still dreaming. The leaf felt as soft as a feather, and the book felt warm and alive, just as I remembered it.

So then, if the dream was real . . .

Trembling, I lifted my hand to my neck and found that the growth was gone. Nothing bulbous and rough was there, only a small curved scar. As I passed my finger across the scar in disbelief, I caught the smell of lilies coming through the window while the stars glistened high above me in the velvety black sky.

CHAPTER SIX

Thorns

The next morning when I got up, my ankle was still throbbing and swollen, the scratches on my face still stung, my leg muscles still ached, and the strap on my backpack was still ripped. When I tried to stand, I winced in pain. I didn't know how I was even going to make it downstairs, let alone trek along some steep mountain trail toward a distant city. And by the looks of how high the sun was, I'd also be late for breakfast and have to listen to Tobal say I told you so.

I sighed.

I guess maybe I'd thought that after my mysterious dream the night before, everything in my life would just get better all at once. Apparently everything wasn't going to be healed by just one dream.

But then I felt my neck. Still healed. And the growth was gone. At least that was good news.

Sore as my ankle was, it took me nearly ten minutes to hobble down the stairs to the dining room, which was empty except for one person: Reyhan was sitting at a table balancing the inn's ledger. When she heard me enter she looked up from her work. "You're late," she said matter-of-factly.

"I had a dream last night," I told her, trusting she would understand the significance of the simple statement.

She looked at my neck and nodded. "I see."

"Afterward I didn't sleep too well. I guess I was so tired I got up a little late."

I hoped she might offer me some breakfast, but she said instead, "So, tell me about your dream."

I recounted my dream and then asked if everyone dreamt the same things here at her inn. She shook her head no.

"But what does my dream mean?" I asked.

Reyhan laughed a little. "We aren't given dreams so we can define them, Kadin, but so that we can see truth from another angle."

"But how can we know the truth if we can't define it?"

Reyhan set down her writing quill. "I heard a story once about a musician, a flutist. She was truly magnificent, inspired, and one day she performed before the king. After her performance, he was stunned and said to her, 'Your song, your music—it moved me. It was powerful. But I have one question: what did it mean?' And the flutist replied, 'Your Majesty, if I could tell you what the song meant, I wouldn't have had to play it.'"

When Reyhan finished her story, she looked at me expectantly for a response.

"I'm not sure I understand," I confessed.

I thought she might lose her patience with me, but she didn't. "If the one who sends dreams could simply tell you what they meant, he wouldn't have to show you," she said.

I considered that for moment. "So, who is he? This one who sends dreams?"

"That is the question, isn't it?" She turned her attention back to her papers. "Why don't you go and get cleaned up, Kadin. There's a bathing pool in the garden."

I took a few hesitant steps and then asked her, "Any chance I could have some breakfast?"

"Too late for breakfast," she responded without looking up. "If you're hungry, lunch is at noon and—"

"I know, I know—don't be late."

◆ ◆ ◆ ◆

I hobbled outside into a lush courtyard surrounded by impassive wooden walls at least twice the height of a man. I imagined the walls had to be that tall to protect the guests from the baron's archers, or perhaps to keep out the beasts that might be prowling these forests.

Even though it was late autumn in the hills all around us, the flowers in the courtyard were in full bloom, bursting with vibrant colors. In the middle of the garden behind a series of hedges, which I assumed had been planted to provide some privacy for the bathers, I heard water splashing. To my right, at the far end of the courtyard, was an immense door held shut by an intricate array of interconnected bolts and locks.

The pathway to Celestia, to the land of the ancient kings.

I followed the stone path to the middle of the courtyard. As I rounded the bend I heard splashing again behind the hedge and, not wanting to walk in on someone taking a bath, I called, "Hello? Anybody in there?"

"I am!" It was Leira's voice. "Stay there. I'll be done in a minute."

"Okay," I said to the hedge. I waited obediently as the splashing stopped. "I didn't know anyone was here. Reyhan suggested I might need a bath."

"Well, she was right about that," said the hedge. "You smell like a swamp. Just a minute. I'm almost done."

After a little while the hedge told me it was okay to come forward, and I stepped around the corner. Leira was standing beside the pool wearing the same clothes she'd had on the night before, drying her hair. I stared at her for a moment. "Your face," I muttered.

"What about my face?" she said defensively.

"Your bruises . . . they're gone."

"What?" Her expression softened a little. She lifted her hand to her chin, felt along her cheekbone, across the bridge of her nose, and then around her eyes. "The water," she whispered. "Tobal said it would help me feel better, but I had no idea."

Without the bruises and dirt covering her face, Leira truly was lovely. Her delicate nose, high cheekbones, and full lips made her look like the princesses pictured in the faery-tale books I'd read as a child.

After a moment, she caught me staring at her. "What's wrong?"

"No. I . . . um . . . your face . . . it looks . . ."

She threw her hands to her hips. "It looks what?"

"Good," I said at last. "It looks good."

"Oh," she replied, with a hint of a blush. "Thank you."

A pause, then I said, "The growth is gone from my neck."

"So is mine." She finished with her hair and twisted the towel around her head. "I had an amazing dream last night . . ." Her voice trailed off.

"Me too."

I wondered what Leira's dream had been about, or if maybe it had been the same as mine, but before I could ask her, she stepped past me.

"It's all yours," she said. "I hope it works on swamp odor as well as it does on bruises."

"Thanks for that."

"Anytime."

"See you later."

"Okay."

After she'd left, I got undressed and slipped into the water. The pool felt cool and refreshing and tingly; almost like the tiny waves were massaging my aching muscles and pulling the pain from me one ripple at a time. I washed until the cuts on my arm and the swelling in my ankle disappeared. It didn't take long. Then I washed until the smell of the marsh was gone from my hair. That took a little longer.

When I was done, I rested in the water for a while, dozing, relaxing, daydreaming, until I heard someone on the other side of the hedge clear his throat.

"There are other guests here too," he said gruffly.

"Oh, sorry." I didn't recognize the voice. "I'll be right out."

I climbed out, dried off, pulled on my clothes, and apologized to the man behind the hedge for taking so long. "I lost track of the time, I guess."

"Understandable." He didn't sound upset anymore. "I just thought I'd enjoy a nice refreshing afternoon bath."

"*Afternoon* bath? You mean lunch is over?"

"About half an hour ago."

Wonderful.

I headed inside and found Tobal standing in the corner of the dining room, his arms folded. "Reyhan told me you'd be late," he said before I could say a word. He stepped into the kitchen and returned with a hearty bowl of landis-root stew and a plate containing a slab of warm homemade bread dripping with melted butter and honey. He set the food on the table near the fireplace. The still-warm stew sent small puffs of steam into the air. He poured me a mug of ale from a chilled pitcher and motioned for me to sit. "You can thank me later," he said good-naturedly.

"I will." Greedily, I bit off a hunk of fresh bread.

"Maybe after you miss supper tonight."

"Wery fummy." I swallowed my mouthful of food. He turned to leave, but before he could walk off I called him back. "Tobal, I've been wondering—the man from the baron's castle, the archer—why did he try to kill me?"

"You were trying to escape the baron's domain."

"But when I was in Abaddon, everyone spoke highly of the baron. They said he was noble, trustworthy, that he took good care of us. Was it all lies?"

"That much of it was. I have a feeling that up here in the hills you're going to find out that many of the things you believed to be true, aren't; and that much of what you thought couldn't possibly be true, is. Baron Dorjan would do anything to keep you in the valley under his rule. Of course, you were easy enough to track . . ."

"The ditheathe?" I was munching on the warm bread. "The thmell?"

"Yes. And stop talking with food in your mouth."

I swallowed. "Sorry. Is there a name for it? For the disease?"

"I'm not a doctor, Kadin, just a doorkeeper. I don't know what it's called, just what it smells like." He turned to leave again.

"So on the other side of the pass where the trail continues—will it be safer there?"

Tobal looked back at me one more time and shook his head. "No. But then, life's not meant to be safe, is it?"

"No," I said slowly. "I guess not." A week ago I never would have said that.

He winked. "Especially not for you. Enjoy your meal."

I wanted to ask him where the book really came from, why it seemed to inhale and exhale in my hand, and how the blood on its cover came to be replaced by a leaf because of a dream. I wanted to ask him so many things, but he walked away before I could say another word.

I had no idea how long I would be welcome to stay here—I had a feeling I could stay for a while, but I was anxious to get on with my journey to Celestia. So, as soon as I finished the meal, I went upstairs to pack my things.

Someone had placed a new coat on the bed in my room. The beige fabric was tightly woven and lightweight, similar to the garb Alcion the wizard had been wearing when I met him in Abaddon. A note lay on top of the coat: *"Compliments of Reyhan."* Beside the coat lay sacks of flour and dried fruits and meat. It looked like enough food for several weeks of hiking. I didn't think I'd need nearly that much but stowed as much as I could in my pack.

Then I spent the rest of the afternoon fixing the strap on my backpack with a needle and thread that Tobal was kind enough to get for me. It wasn't the prettiest sewing job, but I figured it would hold. I just hoped he wouldn't see it and comment on my mending prowess.

I even made it downstairs to the dining room in time for supper. I was ready to gloat to Tobal, but he wasn't there. Apparently he had other duties to attend to besides ridiculing me. Too bad.

At supper I noticed that Leira was wearing a new tunic that appeared to be made from the same fabric as the coat I'd been given. I said hi to her, and she nodded to me and whispered, "Well, at least you smell a little better."

"Glad you noticed."

"Hard not to." In contrast to last night's tears, I was glad to see a glimmer of a smile.

After supper I went to bed early. After all, I had a big day ahead of me.

◆ ◆ ◆ ◆

The next morning I awoke with the sun and slipped on the new coat. It fit perfectly. I left a note of thanks to Reyhan as well as a pile of coins that I thought should cover the expenses from my stay—I left a little extra to pay for the arrow damage and claw marks on the front door.

Then I headed downstairs. I hoped I'd find a cook or steward awake at this hour who could verify that the door I'd seen at the far side of the courtyard led to Celestia, and was surprised to find Reyhan the innkeeper waiting for me at the base of the stairs.

"I hope you weren't planning on leaving without saying goodbye?" she said.

"I didn't want to wake anyone."

"Well, there was someone already awake." She motioned toward the dining room. I thought it was probably Tobal, but instead Leira appeared, outfitted with a pack of her own.

"You wanted me to wait around for him?" Leira scoffed lightly.

"I've been keeping her here for almost half an hour," Reyhan told me. "It wasn't easy."

"I can only imagine," I said.

"So you really want us to travel together?" Leira said.

"My dear, look at the boy. How far do you think he would make it without your help?"

A smile flickered across Leira's face. "Good point."

"Thanks a lot," I replied.

"You need each other," Reyhan said, then gestured toward my pack. "After all, you have the map."

"There's a map?" Leira exclaimed.

I pulled off my pack and produced the Book of Blood. "Flip it open," Reyhan said, "to the end."

I did as I was told and stared at the strange squibbles and indecipherable writing. Once again I wished I knew how to read the second half of this book.

"Do you know how to read Serecean?" Reyhan asked me.

I shook my head.

"Serecean?" Leira stepped forward and peered at the book's pages. "I know Serecean."

What?

She proved herself by pointing out landmarks within the book and naming mountains in a tongue I couldn't understand.

"See?" Reyhan smiled. "You have the maps, and she knows how to read them. You two need each other."

I wasn't quite ready to say I *needed* Leira, but looking at her now that she was cleaned up I could think of worse people to be stuck traveling with.

"How do you know how to read that?" I asked her.

"Oh, I'm full of surprises."

I had no idea how to respond to that.

"So," Reyhan said, "it looks like you two will have to stick together, or you both may get lost."

"Or I could just steal the book from him when he's asleep," Leira said slyly. I'm pretty sure she was kidding. "I've noticed he likes to sleep in late."

Reyhan tilted her head at me. "Kadin, you'll have to watch yourself then. Keep an eye on her."

I could also think of worse people to have to keep an eye on. "I will."

I shook Reyhan's hand. "I left you some money on the bed in my room. I hope it'll be enough."

"I'm sure that it's plenty. Thank you." She led Leira and I outside to the courtyard. "Now, one last thing. I wouldn't want you to leave without these." Reyhan handed each of us a parchment tied with a crimson thread. Each scroll was held shut by a small round seal of melted wax with an elaborate letter C imprinted in it.

"What are they?" Leira asked.

"Pardons from King Kiral. They bear the seal of Celestia and will assure your entrance into the city. The pardons cover all the crimes you committed while in Abaddon, and the ones you may commit on the way to his palace." She became serious for a moment. "You do know what deeds I speak of, don't you? From your dreams?"

"Yes," Leira said slowly.

Maybe she did have the same dream I had.

I gently slid the pardon into my pocket. "I think I can speak for Leira when I say we don't intend to break any of King Kiral's laws on the way to Celestia."

"No one ever intends to," Reyhan sighed. "They just do." Then she spun and exclaimed, "Ah. Tobal!"

He'd arrived in the courtyard while we were talking. Reyhan waved for him to join us. "I can't open the door for you." She gestured toward the intricate locks. "Only Tobal knows the combination."

He stepped past us and began to expertly unlock the series of bolts and latches. "Each has to be done in order," he explained as he clicked through the combination, "or the next one won't work." At last he looked up at a guard stationed on a nearby tower. The man signaled that all was clear. Tobal only had one bolt left.

"All right then," I said. "Well, thank you, Reyhan, Tobal. Thank you both very much. I can see I have a lot to learn about this new land, this life of a traveler—"

"Vagabond," Tobal corrected me. "We prefer to call those who seek Celestia *vagabonds.*"

"Vagabond." Leira nodded. "I like that."

"All right then," I corrected myself. "This life of a vagabond."

Tobal ceremoniously threw back the last bolt and reached for the handle.

I couldn't wait. This would be my first glimpse of Celestia, perhaps on the next ridge.

But as he swung the door open, I caught my breath. There were no mountains in sight. There was no city. Just a narrow path leading into a dark thicket.

On this side of the pass, the vegetation was much different than the towering trees on the path I'd taken to get here. Most of the underbrush was scraggly and thick, and every so often a charred stump rose from the thicket. The undergrowth was filled with glistening thistles and tangled thorns.

"There was a fire here some years ago," Tobal explained. "The land is still recovering." He pointed to the pathway. "You'll see other trails intersect this one, but don't follow them. There's only one way to the city. You may hear voices whispering from the thicket, but don't listen to them." As he spoke, some of the thorns appeared to move on their own, snaking toward us and then curling back with a thin clatter into the thicket.

Just like the thorns in my dream.

"Are they alive?" Leira asked Tobal nervously.

"Of course."

"No," she said, "I mean *alive.*"

Reyhan answered for him. "Yes. Of course."

"I think I dreamt of this," I whispered. The call of a raptor high above the tangled forest echoed eerily through the morning.

"Um," Leira said hesitantly. "Are there any dogs on this side of the ridge?"

"Dogs?" Reyhan said. "No, not usually."

"Good."

"Just packs of bloodthirsty wolves."

Both Leira and I watched Reyhan to see if she was joking, but she gave no indication that she was. "Oh," Leira said. "How nice."

"Stay on the path, Kadin." Tobal patted me on the shoulder. "And even you'll be able to make it."

We all said our goodbyes, Tobal swung the door shut behind us, and Leira and I started up the narrow trail cut into the forest of living thorns.

CHAPTER SEVEN

Companions

As we entered the tangled woods, the brambles at the edge of the trail slithered and writhed before us. A few times when the trail became especially narrow, I accidentally stepped too close to the thorns. They quickly came to life, snapping and untangling, trying to wrap around my ankles and draw me in. Once, they almost succeeded.

The day became misty, like the meadow in my dream.

As we hiked, I kept expecting the trail to become easier, the pathway smoother. But if anything, it became more and more crowded by the thorns and even harder to follow.

After we'd been walking for what seemed like hours with no change whatsoever in the scenery, Leira asked, "How long is it supposed to be like this?"

"I don't know. Tobal said there was a fire. It might have swept through this whole region."

She eyed the underbrush. "I hope the trail gets a little easier soon."

"Me too."

At times the path became so narrow that I thought maybe we'd lost our way. But that didn't seem possible, considering how few other trails we saw and how straight this one went relentlessly uphill.

We walked in relative silence most of the day. Leira seemed to have a lot on her mind, and I didn't really want to bother her. I had no way of knowing what had happened to her in the baron's castle, but I figured the least I could do was give her some space to sort things out.

Eventually I began to wonder how a road that was supposed to lead to freedom could be so narrow and precarious. It didn't make sense. Most of the time we couldn't even walk beside each other and had to take turns leading the way. I couldn't help but wonder why, if the king really wanted people to walk this trail, he didn't clear away the thorns.

That day passed. And the next. Then the next. We eased into a rhythm of hiking, eating, and sleeping. Days began to flow past us with the miles. Our muscles grew wiry and strong. The path we were on eventually flattened out but remained overgrown and wild. Sometimes we would see flickers of gray and white flash through the thicket as beasts ran past us in search of prey. Based on what Reyhan had said before we left the inn, I assumed the predators were wolves, but it was hard to tell since they never crossed the trail itself, just stayed hidden in the scrub brush and thorns. Ravens called from high above us, and hawks regularly circled the charred, thorny forest in search of food.

At times the distant mountains seemed to get closer, but mostly everything stayed pretty much the same. Leira and I didn't talk too much, but with time the silence became less and less awkward, and the distance between us seemed less and less formidable, until it almost seemed like we could read each other's mind.

Each night I heard her crying before going to sleep.

One day we came to a lake beside the trail. We hadn't had a chance to bathe in days and took turns swimming in the cold, brisk water.

While Leira swam, I took everything out of my pack to air out. When she'd finished and was toweling off her hair, she noticed the coil of rope beside my pack. "What's that for?"

"The shepherd gave it to me. He told me that when the time came I'd know what to do with it."

"Hmm," she said, "the shepherd.

"You met him too?"

"Indeed," she said, echoing his favorite word. "But only briefly." She finished drying her hair, and I stuffed the rope back into my pack, then we gathered everything up and headed on our way again, refreshed and, best of all, clean.

That was the day I asked Leira what had happened to her at the baron's castle.

We'd left the lake and hiked about two miles when the path became wider and we could finally walk together side by side in relative ease. "Leira, can I ask you something? Something personal?"

"What is it?"

I was a little hesitant to even bring it up. "Um . . . why did you leave Abaddon? Was it the baron? Did he call for you?"

She shook her head. "It wasn't like that. I met up with a man named Alcion—"

"Alcion!" I exclaimed. "He's the one who gave me the book. I didn't know he'd been to Abaddon before."

Leira shrugged. "I just know I met him about a year ago. He gave me an invitation that he said came from King Kiral himself. According to Alcion, the king wanted to adopt me."

"Adopt you?"

"That's what he said. As you remember, both my parents died when I was very young."

"Yes. A fire."

"Right. Well, I was living with my aunt when Alcion came. She was terrible. Never home. And when she was, her boyfriends would hit me. She never even tried to stop them. Just told me to deal with it, to grow up. Nearly every day I thought about running away."

"Why did you stay?"

"I was afraid to leave and I didn't have anywhere else to go. So, when Alcion said the king had chosen me to become a princess you can imagine how skeptical I was."

"It would be hard for anyone to believe."

"Right. Why would the king have chosen me? And how could he have even heard of me, living in a small town so far from his land? It didn't make any sense." She paused. "But it is every girl's dream, though—to one day find out that you're really a princess."

I stepped away from an angry branch reaching for my leg. "So I've heard."

"The night after I met Alcion I had a dream that all the dark thoughts I'd ever had and all the evil things I'd ever done were written on a scroll. As the scroll was being unrolled, two horrible forms appeared beside my bed. They looked like ghouls with human skin stretched across their faces. One of them turned to the other and said, 'What should we do with her?' And the other said, 'If she keeps on like this we may just lose her.' And the first one replied, 'Bring out the chains.' And that's when I woke up."

"Whoa."

"That's what I thought. I was afraid those two things would return when I was *awake,* so the next day I begged Alcion to help me. That's when he showed me where my name appears in the Book of Blood."

I stared at her. "Your name is in the Book of Blood!"

She nodded. "Yes. I'll show it to you the next time we stop. Anyway, I finally believed Alcion, and I decided to leave. He had a whole pile of invitations that he delivered on that trip, but as far as I know, I'm the only one who left Abaddon."

I was struck, and for some reason hurt, by the fact that he hadn't given me one of those invitations. "How did you end up at the baron's?"

"On my way to the inn, two of the archers from his castle caught up with me. They told me how wonderful life would be with the baron, how badly he wanted to meet me. Somehow they convinced me that my invitation had come from the baron rather than the king and, in a moment of weakness, I went with them—but of course everything they said was a lie."

"So that's how you knew that archer was trying to trick me too."

"Yes."

I wasn't sure if I should ask the next question but I felt like

I had to know. "Leira, when they took you there, to the castle, what did they do to you?"

She fell silent, her eyes trained straight ahead. "I can't say all the things they did to me, but I'll bet you can guess most of them."

I was quiet.

She wiped her arm across her eyes, which had started to glisten with tears. "They took turns visiting me in the dungeon, the guards did. Even the baron. It seemed to go on forever. Until, finally I escaped."

"How?"

She reached into her hair and produced a hairpin. "I'm pretty good with locks. The shepherd gave this to me, just like he gave you that rope."

"The walking stick too."

She acknowledged that with a nod but said nothing.

After a few minutes I told Leira, "I think Reyhan was right."

"What, that I'm a very foolish young woman?"

"No. That you're a very brave one."

Then she was silent, and we walked together up the trail beneath the late afternoon sun.

◆ ◆ ◆ ◆

The next time we stopped was several hours later when it was getting dark. Up ahead of us we could see that the trail forked off in two distinct directions—one went directly up the ridge; the other disappeared down into a sloping meadow.

A couple of people had set up camp near the crossroads. We'd only met one other person since leaving the inn—about a week ago we'd found her lying fast asleep near the side of the trail. The woman had obviously been sleeping for quite some time since a thick layer of moss was growing on her cheeks and hair. We'd tried to wake her but it was no use.

"This is a strange land indeed," Leira had said.

"Yes it is." I brushed my finger across the sleeping woman's mossy cheek. She'd snored a bit, smiled in her sleep and then rolled over.

But the two men ahead of us now were not asleep; they were laughing uproariously around a blazing campfire. Although they sounded like they were having a good time, I wondered if the pair would be friendly to us or not. For a moment, I wished I had some kind of weapon.

I gripped my walking stick more firmly. "Hello! Are you vagabonds?"

"Yes, yes!" came the reply between bursts of laughter. "On our way to the city of Celestia!"

I felt a wash of relief. "Greetings, then!"

But Leira was less trusting. "Be careful. Remember what happened the last time you talked to someone—the archer, the dogs."

"Right." I studied the pair by the fire for a minute. "We'll be careful, but we have to pass this way. Let's at least talk to them."

As I walked cautiously toward the men, Leira whispered to me, "Do you smell something?"

"No."

"Smell again."

I did. And she was right. I did smell something.

As we approached the two vagabonds, I could see what it was. They were both still infected. The festering sores on their necks were swollen and filled with thick pus. It was so bad Leira asked them if they were okay. The taller of the two assured us he was fine, never felt better, it was a grand night after all, and why didn't we have a seat and join them by the fire?

Although the sores on their necks made me even more wary, neither of the two men appeared to be anything but enthusiastic vagabonds on their way to Celestia. It was too late in the day for Leira and me to decide which trail to take, and the two men were so congenial that after a few minutes, even Leira began to relax, and we rested on the logs by their campfire to eat supper and tell of our journeys.

Our two new friends introduced themselves as Castel and Biminak. Castel was nearly a head taller than me, and lanky, with a thin mustache and wild eyebrows. Biminak was shorter and rounder than any of us. For some reason he reminded me of a muffin. When he laughed, he would inhale instead of exhale so he sounded like he was snorting. Castel took frequent advantage of this, joking and carrying on until Biminak began to snort. Then Castel would break into great whooping laughter, slapping his knees until his eyes watered. They were quite a pair.

"So, tell us about your trip," I said. "How long did you stay at the inn?"

"Oh, no." Castel gave a dismissive wave of his hand. "We came a different way, didn't we, Biminak?"

Castel's chubby friend nodded enthusiastically. "Found another path."

"But I thought you need to pass through the inn?" Leira said. "That there was only one way?"

Castel looked surprised. "Oh, there are lots of ways. I climbed over a wall to get in here. You didn't, though, did you Biminak? That would have been a sight to see—Biminak climbing a wall!"

Biminak grinned large in the firelight. "I took a shortcut."

I shoved a stick into the fire to keep the blaze going. "I didn't think there are any shortcuts to Celestia. The book doesn't mention them, and both the shepherd and Tobal said there's only one way to the city."

Our new friends looked surprised. "Who?" Biminak asked.

"Never heard of 'em," said Castel.

Leira and I told them about the shepherd and the doorkeeper and the owner of the inn, and they stared at us blankly. We spoke of hounds and wolves and dungeons, and they assured us that their path so far had been relatively smooth and easy and free of danger. They could hardly believe all the troubles we'd already faced. They had come from another village in the western plains but hadn't encountered the swamp on the edge of the valley, been chased by dogs, shot at by archers, or anything—but neither had they visited the inn or had any remarkable dreams. And perhaps most importantly, they were still infected and had been given no pardons from the king.

"I think you should go back to the inn," I suggested. "I'm sure they'll be glad to receive you, give you pardons and—"

Castel grunted. "From what you've said that would take weeks." He prodded at the fire. "Much too long."

"Much too long," Biminak echoed.

But Leira agreed with me: "No, really. You need to get rid of those infections on your necks. They look pretty bad."

Risking the chance of offending the two men, I added, "We can smell them, and if we can, so can the animals—the wolves and whatever else roams these hills. They may find you when you're asleep."

As Biminak listened his eyes grew larger and larger until they looked much too big for his head.

Castel noticed. "They're just telling campfire tales, Biminak." He gave his friend a great whack on the shoulder. "Ooh . . ." he said menacingly, "are you afraid of a wolf, Biminak?" Then Castel set about howling like a wolf and Biminak began to shake.

Leira wouldn't give up. "We're not joking around here. You two may be in danger."

With that, Castel whooped out a mighty laugh and fell off his log, clutching his scrawny stomach with both hands. When Biminak saw that, he started snorting.

Leira just shook her head. "I'm going to bed." She walked to the edge of the campfire light and unrolled her blanket.

I stayed up with Castel and Biminak for a few more minutes, but then headed to bed myself when they wouldn't stop howling at each other like wolves. Late into the night I heard them talking and laughing and snorting by the campfire. Occasionally I heard real wolves, or some other type of animal, roaming and panting in the nearby thicket.

◆ ◆ ◆ ◆

In the morning Leira joined me as I sat sipping warm tea. Both Castel and Biminak were still snoring loudly beside the trail. She poured some water to make tea for herself. "I don't think they're taking this trip very seriously."

"They're certainly enjoying themselves," I said noncommittally.

"How could they have found another way here without going through the inn? Doesn't the book say that's where the journey starts?"

I shrugged. "I thought so."

"I don't trust them."

"They seem harmless enough."

She quietly appraised the snoring duo.

"They're nice," I said in their defense.

"Kadin, *nice* isn't enough."

I looked at her concerned face in the early morning light. Her beautiful and yet sad eyes were filled with concern. Though I wanted to give these two men the benefit of the doubt, I had to agree with Leira that we should be wary. "Okay, we'll keep an eye on them. But I think we should travel together." I heard Castel stir, lowered my voice. "There's strength in numbers."

She reluctantly agreed.

Castel looked our way. "Up already?" He groggily rubbed his eyes, then used a stick to prod his friend awake. "Come on, Biminak! Time to wake up." He poked him again. Biminak groaned and rolled over. Castel took to intermittently poking him, just enough to annoy his friend, but not quite enough to rouse him.

It took the two of them another half hour to get dressed and to finish yawning and complaining about how early it was. By then, both Leira and I were packed and anxious to get going. We walked to the other side of the campsite to scout out the trail.

To our left, the path descended into a clearing, bright and sunny. Straight ahead, the trail rose sharply toward the peak of a high mountain, the highest I'd seen yet. The entire way appeared to be swallowed in shadows from the thick, tangled underbrush.

"Okay, Kadin, I think I remember this crossroads from the book," Leira said. "I'm pretty sure our trail goes up that peak and then down into a gorge. Let's check the map."

"Right." I unbuckled the top flap of my pack and fished around for the Book of Blood. "And then you can show me where your name appears."

I pulled one item and then another out of my pack, but the book wasn't there. I scanned the campsite. "I don't understand," I mumbled.

"What is it?"

"The book. It's gone."

"What?"

"Gone."

"Where is it?"

"I don't know." At first I thought maybe Castel or Biminak had snatched it while I slept, but then, with a sinking feeling in my gut, I remembered taking it out of my pack at the lake. "Leira." My voice faltered. "I think I know where it is."

"Where?"

"I left it back by the lake."

"The lake? You've got to be kidding me." I said nothing. Her hands went to her hips. "Kadin, how could you?"

Her tone irritated me. "It's not like I forgot it on purpose. I was in a hurry to get going."

Now it was her turn to be quiet. After a moment she said,

"The only maps we have are in that book."

"I know."

"I didn't memorize them all."

"I know."

"We can't keep going without them."

"I know, that too."

From across the campsite, Castel looked our way suspiciously, though I don't think he'd heard yet what we were talking about.

"Just let me think for a minute," I said to Leira.

Hiking back to the lake would take hours, but I couldn't think of any other viable course of action.

She drummed her hands on her leg as she waited for me to go on. Finally I sighed. "Okay. I guess we're going to have to go back and look for the book."

She rolled her eyes. "I don't believe this."

"What else do you want me to say? I'm sorry. I wasn't careful. But now we've got to go get it."

"Actually, no." She stared at the trail. "*We* don't have to go anywhere. *We* didn't leave the map back there. You did. You go get it."

"Leira, you're coming with me. The innkeeper told me to keep my eye on you."

"Well then, you're going to have to find a way to do that while I wait here with our two new friends." With that, she plopped her pack down and folded her arms.

Great.

"Well, when do we get started?" Biminak asked from the other side of the burned out campfire. He had his pack on. He seemed clueless about the conversation Leira and I had just had.

I took a deep breath. "Castel, Biminak, it looks like I forgot something a few miles back—the book with our maps. I'm heading back to go get it. I'll hurry. I promise. I shouldn't be more than a few hours. Leira's going to stay here with you."

Leira grunted.

Castel started laughing. "You forgot your maps? Oh that's great! That's perfect! Did you hear that, Biminak?" Castel began slapping his knees. "He forgot his book of maps!"

It really wasn't all that funny.

Biminak beamed. "In that case. I don't mind if I rest just a bit longer." He threw his pack down and began to unroll his blanket.

"Just hurry," Leira said, rubbing her forehead.

"I will," I said.

And I did.

◆ ◆ ◆ ◆

I wish I could say that the trip down to the lake was as enjoyable as the hike from it. But it wasn't. Overall I was pretty miserable. The whole way I felt like I'd wasted both my time and Leira's—even Castel's and Biminak's. I kept trying to tell myself that it was an honest mistake, that anyone could have misplaced the book, but it didn't seem to help. I still felt disappointed with myself and frustrated.

As soon as the lake came into view, I hurried even faster. Thankfully, without having to backtrack over all the places we'd explored around the shore, I found the book in the grass right where I'd pulled everything out of my pack.

"Thank you," I whispered to no one in particular.

You're welcome, I heard, as if someone were whispering in my ear.

I looked around, but no one was there.

Unsettled that I was hearing things, but glad to have found the Book of Blood, I picked it up and started back up the trail I'd just come down.

Since I didn't really like the idea of leaving Leira alone with Castel and Biminak, I went as fast as I could. But the trail was all uphill from this direction, and it was midway through the afternoon when I finally arrived at the crossroads again.

Ahead of me were the smoldering campfire and the flattened grass where we'd slept the night before. Leira's pack lay next to mine, but other than that, the campsite was deserted.

"Leira?" I scanned the nearby thicket for any sign of her. "Leira? Where are you? Castel? Biminak?"

The only reply I heard was a growl in the underbrush. It sounded close. I clutched the walking stick, took a step toward it and called again, "Leira!"

CHAPTER EIGHT

Descent

In the tangled thicket just a few feet away from me, I saw the face of a frightening beast. To call it a wolf would be an insult to all natural wolves. Everything about this creature was monstrous. Its eyes gleamed with a terrible knowing intelligence. It snarled at me, revealing a mouth full of dagger-like teeth.

"Back!" I cried.

It didn't retreat, but it didn't seem to be coming any closer either. After a moment, it sniffed at the breeze, but must not have been interested in me because it bounded off. Apparently, it was tracking something else.

I could only wonder what. Or who.

"Leira!" I tossed the book to the ground and jogged up the trail. "Castel! Biminak!"

I had no way to tell how far my voice would carry in the thicket, but I called again, even louder. "Leira! Where are you?"

Wind blew lazily across the clearing, bringing me no answer.

"Leira!"

Just as I was beginning to get desperate, I heard her voice, faint, but recognizable, ahead of me on the trail. "Up here, Kadin!"

I ran toward her, still worried, my heart hammering in my chest.

At last I caught sight of her coming my way, picking her way down the path. She'd hiked to the top of the peak by following the trail that led up the ridge.

"Are you okay?" I yelled.

"Yes, I'm fine."

"Where are Castel and Biminak?"

After a momentary pause, she replied, "They left."

"What do you mean? They just left you here alone!"

By then she'd come close enough so that she didn't need to yell anymore. "We heard noises, Kadin. Wolves, I guess. They got closer and closer, and Castel and Biminak panicked. Castel yelled at Biminak for a while, and then they both took off. The last I saw of them they were heading down the trail over there, the one to the open fields."

That was the direction the wolf I'd just seen had headed.

As Leira approached me, she pointed up the mountain. "I went up there to see if I could locate them, but I haven't been able to. Then I heard you calling."

"I can't believe they left you alone."

"I can take care of myself," she said firmly as we finally met at the crossroads.

"I didn't mean it that way, I'm just . . ." *Concerned about you.* ". . . glad you're all right."

She gazed at the field. "I hope they are too."

I was quiet for a moment. "There's not much we can do about it now."

She said nothing.

"I think we should get going."

At last she looked my way. "Did you find the book?"

"I set it by my pack."

Leira headed toward it, then checked the map carefully. Once she was assured that the pathway up the mountain was the one we wanted, we took off.

The view at the summit was stunning. Along the horizon in every direction, mountain peaks climbed toward the clouds.

But I still saw no sign of Celestia to the land of the ancient kings.

"We go down," Leira said.

I peered down the gorge slicing between the mountains. In the last few weeks of hiking I'd learned that sometimes going downhill is tougher and more dangerous than climbing uphill. In this case the trail looked impossibly steep and precarious.

"Are you sure?"

She showed me the map. (She'd understandably demanded to carry the book for a while, and I hadn't argued with her.) "We descend a few hundred feet, then we follow a river." Far below us I could hear the rush of water where all the streams from the adjoining mountains converged into one.

"But that doesn't make any sense," I objected. "We've climbed this far up only to descend again? There's got to be another way. A ridge or something."

Leira looked intently at the map, traced a line with her finger, then scrutinized the actual terrain surrounding us. "This is right, Kadin. The map says we have to go through this gorge. Besides, there aren't any other trails around here to take."

"But look at those cliffs." I indicated toward the sheer rock faces on the mountains across the valley. "If we go down, who knows if we'll ever make it up again. Couldn't we just bushwhack along this ridge and then, if we have to, descend sometime later? I mean, it looks like there might be a game trail along—"

"Now you're starting to sound like Castel. Besides, you're the one who keeps telling me we have to follow the map." She pointed at some of the meaningless squiggles on the page. "Here. See? We have to travel down the gorge, and then . . . well, from then on, it's a little unclear."

"A little unclear."

"Yes."

"And what does that mean? Exactly?"

She drew my attention to a thick curling figure that looked like a backward *N* with an *8* running through the middle of it. "This symbol here means 'crossing over.' Most of the time it means 'deliverance,' but . . ."

"But what?"

"But sometimes it's used for 'death.'"

"Well, that's reassuring."

I studied the steep ravine. It looked to me as though we'd have to travel downstream for several miles, and then at the other end of the gorge, scale one of the rock faces to get past the next mountain range.

She took the lead. "Come on. It can't be that bad."

But it was.

With every step, my feet slid on the scree-covered trail, at times sending rocks plummeting hundreds of feet down into the throat of the gorge. Rather than switch back and forth down the incline to make the walking easier, the trail we were on seemed to head straight down.

"Watch your step," I cautioned her.

"I'll keep that in mind."

Twilight settled over the mountains, but the path was too steep and precarious to set up camp, so we pressed on. Several times I tried to use the walking stick to steady myself, but it kept sliding across the rocks or getting caught between them and throwing me off balance. One time in anger and exasperation, I nearly flung it out as far as I could into the gorge but caught myself just in time.

The minutes passed by agonizingly slowly.

Once in a while I heard Leira whisper something under her breath. It sounded like the same angry words I was thinking but simply hadn't said. Darkness came. The stars emerged. And we hiked. Mixed in with the sound of rushing water were the howls of wolves from the ridgeline.

By the time we reached the river, we were both completely exhausted. I felt like kissing that first patch of ground that was actually flat enough to sleep on. Leira collected water from the river while I made us some flatbread on a small campfire. After eating a quiet supper together, we both collapsed into our bedrolls.

The next morning I was a little grumpy and very sore. Leira pulled out a small flask and carefully poured a few drops of water onto her hand and then massaged them onto her left shoulder.

I sat up, barely kept from groaning. "What's that?"

"Reyhan let me bring some of the water from the bath. She said to use it sparingly."

Healing water!

"Great. I suppose I could try just a little."

"Oh really? Are you sore, Kadin?"

I opened my mouth to say that of course I was sore, how could anyone not be sore after a hike like that—but then my male instincts kicked in. "Sore? Oh, um, yeah . . . I'm fine."

She smiled sweetly. "Good. Then we can save the rest for when we really need it." After screwing on the lid, she slipped the flask into her pack, flexed the healed muscles of her shoulder, and went to get some food from my backpack.

When she wasn't looking I collapsed back to the ground.

A few minutes later she brought the Book of Blood to me. "If you carry this, we'll still need each other." I took her offer to mean that she'd forgiven me for leaving it behind earlier.

"Thanks."

The sun was already blazing above us, but it was still cool in the gorge. Here, once again, the hills were forested, and I was glad to be leaving the thorns behind. As I grabbed the walking stick, Leira noticed the arrowhead and short length of broken-off arrow shaft sticking out of it.

"I've been meaning to ask you. How did that happen, anyway? Was it at the inn?"

I turned the staff so I could see the arrowhead and began to explain how I'd been fighting the dogs when the archer shot at me, but while I told her the story I inadvertently positioned the walking stick so that the carved face on top stared directly at the sun. The two eyes inset in the bird's face began to glow as they captured the sun's rays and then channeled the reflection of the sunlight into two narrow beams. The beams converged and met in a tree about fifty feet away. The dead autumn leaves still hanging from the tree burst into flame.

"What are you doing!" Leira cried.

"I have no idea." I dropped the stick to the ground and stared at the tree, hoping it wouldn't set the whole forest on fire. Thankfully, only a few leaves had caught fire. And they quickly burned out.

Leira eyed me. "Can you do that again?"

"I'm not sure I want to."

"Go on. See if you can. We might be able to use it against the wolves if they follow us."

I picked up the walking stick and turned it so that the bird's eyes faced the sun again. It took me a while to get the angle right, but at last I did, and the two streaks of light appeared. This time I was careful to direct them into our campfire pit. The embers sizzled and blazed up in flames. "Okay," I said, "so I guess I can start fires with this walking stick. The shepherd told me this stick would serve me well, but I had no idea."

Carefully, I turned the face of the bird away from the sun, the streaks of light disappeared, and Leira inspected the carved words along the walking stick's shaft. "Do you know what those words mean?"

"The shepherd didn't tell me."

She trailed her finger down the stick, mouthing Serecean words as she did. *"From the ashes,"* she whispered, *"new life will arise."*

"The ashes? What ashes?"

"Well, it's obvious. You know what kind of bird that is on the top, don't you?"

I shook my head. "An eagle? Maybe a hawk?"

"It's a phoenix. A bird that dies and then rises to life again from its own ashes."

I stared up at her curiously. "How do you know all this stuff?"

"It's kind of a long story."

I waited, but she didn't elaborate, just handed the stick back to me. I touched one of the jeweled eyes of the phoenix. "I wonder why the shepherd gave it to me?"

"I don't know." Leira glanced at the tree with the scorched

leaves. "But be careful with that thing. I don't want you to go starting any fires that you can't put out."

◆ ◆ ◆ ◆

Neither of us much liked the idea of following the river further into the valley, but in the end we decided we'd be in more trouble if we went our own way instead of trusting the map.

So, for the next two days, we descended.

On each side of us, the mountains rose steeply toward the sky. In some places, rock faces jutted out of the cliffs and towered thousands of feet straight above us. Eventually, as the ground leveled off, the river slowed and widened. But instead of finding ourselves in a floodplain, a mountain range stretched before us.

"Leira, what do you think—does the river empty into a lake, or bend around that mountain?"

She studied the terrain for a moment. "I don't know. There doesn't seem to be enough room for a lake—but that's not my biggest concern."

"What is?"

She gazed up at the ridgeline high above us. "I get the feeling we're being followed. Last night I could have sworn I heard horses. I've been hearing them again over the last hour or so."

"Why didn't you say anything?"

"I wasn't sure before—" Her voice was low. "—but now . . ."

I listened intently. "I don't hear anything."

"And you didn't smell that marsh water in your hair either."

"Okay, so maybe my senses aren't as acute as yours—"

"Did you say I have cute senses?" she said lightly.

"Um, *acute*," I clarified. "Your senses are acute. Anyway, are you sure it was a horse? Maybe it's just Castel and Biminak wandering around up there, and you heard Biminak laughing."

"I heard a horse whinny, Kadin."

"I'd say that's a pretty good description of Biminak's laughter."

She shook her head. "You're impossible." The mood had softened some, but she still looked concerned.

"We'll stop and listen every couple minutes," I offered. "Keep an eye on the ridgeline."

That satisfied her, and as we traveled on, both of us listened for any sound of horses, both of us scanned the ridge, but we heard nothing, saw nothing, and eventually she admitted that she might have been hearing things after all.

At times we lost the trail as it crisscrossed back and forth across the stream, but then we'd pick it up again a few hundred paces later. At one point I was wondering if we might have lost track of it for good when Leira stopped abruptly in front of me, and I almost ran into her.

"Kadin, the river doesn't empty into a lake," she whispered.

"How can you be sure?"

"Because it empties into a mountain."

"What?"

She pointed. Ahead of us, the mountains between which we'd been walking came together, creating a pass only a few hundred feet above the river. And rather than feeding into a lake or coursing around the side of one of the mountains, the river simply emptied into an enormous cave at the base of the pass.

"'Crossing over,'" she said. "The only way to cross over to the other side of this mountain range is to go *under* it."

"Deliverance," I said.

"Or death." She finished my thought for me. I wasn't exactly glad that she had.

The river, which had at times been deep, spread out, becoming shallower here in the level ground between us and the cave. Debris washed high against the trees told me that at times the river had flooded this valley, but apparently since it was late autumn, the water was at a relatively low level, even slowing to a trickle in places.

When we were about a hundred paces from the cave's entrance, Leira stopped in her tracks. "Kadin, what are those?" With a trembling finger she pointed toward something sticking out of the mud not far ahead of us.

"Sticks," I said. "Bleached white by the sun. Probably washed down here during flood season from higher up in the gorge."

She walked a little further and then froze again. "They're not sticks, Kadin."

Lying half-covered in mud at her feet was a human skull.

"Oh," I murmured. "Bones."

Scattered piles of human remains greeted us. Some of the bones lay upright, gripped in the mud of the slow-moving river; others had washed into gruesome stacks against boulders or downed trees during seasons when the river had been high.

"What happened here?" Leira whispered.

"Something bad."

"Very bad."

I thought of the eyes of the phoenix head, perhaps the only real weapon we had with us, but clouds had covered the sun, rendering the stick, at least for the moment, useless.

Everything seemed eerily quiet. Not even a bird's song broke the silence. The river flowed by noiselessly.

"I don't like it here," Leira said.

"Me neither." Hoping to find a route past the cave, I studied the steep cliffs surrounding us, boxing us in. Unfortunately, it didn't look like we'd be able to climb up or scramble over the pass. "It looks like we either have to backtrack or go through that cave."

As we stepped forward, a low rumbling sound came from the grotto's opening.

"Okay. Let's go back," she whispered. "You were probably right; I made a mistake reading the map."

The cave became quiet, but I heard sounds above us on the mountain pass. "I don't know, I—"

Then I heard it. A horse.

I looked up.

Two riders appeared.

"Hullo, vagabonds!" called one of the men in a high-pitched, sarcastic voice.

"It's them," Leira gasped.

"Who? Castel and Biminak?"

"No. Guards. From the baron's castle. I'd know that voice anywhere."

"It can't be."

"Leeeeeeira," taunted the high-pitched voice. "Remember me? I'm sure you do." Both men croaked with horrible laughter that echoed throughout the valley. Even their horses whinnied and neighed as if they were laughing themselves.

I felt a surge of anger, the deep desire to protect Leira.

Almost imperceptibly, her hands began to twitch. The healing waters at the inn may have cured her body, but they hadn't purged her soul of the memories of those days in the baron's dungeon, suffering at the hands of these men.

I willed the sun to come out so I could use the phoenix head of the staff, but it remained hidden behind the clouds.

Ahead of us, something large moved inside the cave. Whatever lived in there had awakened.

This was not good.

"And you—Kadin!" the other guard yelled to me. In contrast to his partner's, this man's voice was gruff and angry rather than tight and sarcastic. "You cracked the skull of one of our wolfhounds. He died a week after you beat him with that stick.

"Too bad I was a little slow with those other two."

A grim silence followed my words.

I looked at the steep cliffs on each side of us. There was no way up. If these men were archers, they could easily stop our retreat up the riverbed with a barrage of arrows. The only other direction we could go was into the cave.

I thought that buying a little time might give me a chance to find an escape route.

"How did you find us?" I yelled.

The high-pitched one replied. "Your friends helped us. We just followed them through the fields and then killed a couple of wolves who'd surrounded them."

"Castel and Biminak," Leira whispered.

"With a little persuasion the fat one told us everything we needed to know."

I couldn't stand to think of what these two sadistic archers had done to those two men.

One of them launched a round object down the ravine. It careened down the hill, then landed with a sickening crunch and rolled to a stop near my feet.

Biminak's lifeless eyes stared up at me, his mouth frozen in a horrible gasp of pain.

"No!" Leira staggered backward. I wrapped an arm around her, then led her past the horrid thing. I couldn't stand to touch it or even nudge it out of the way with my foot.

"What do you want with us?" Leira screamed.

"The baron sent us to give you one last chance," the gruff one replied. "Although if it were up to me your chances would be up."

"Except for the girl," the whiny one cut in. "I could still have some fun with her. Leave her for me."

I wondered if any of the bones around us were sharp enough for me to use as a dagger to use when they came for us. I held Leira close. Scrutinized the riverbed.

Saw nothing that would serve as a weapon.

"I'm not going back, Kadin," Leira whispered. "I couldn't—"

"Don't worry. I won't let them take you."

"Promise me."

"I promise."

"Promise me you'll do whatever you need to do to stop them."

"Of course."

"*Whatever* you need to do."

A chill gripped me. "What are you saying, Leira?"

But before she could answer, the angry-sounding guard dismounted and walked to the very edge of the precipice. "Baron Dorjan offers you a deal," he said evenly. "A deal, I might add, you won't get from the king you seem to be in such a hurry to meet."

"We'll never go with you," I called. No sharp bones. No discarded swords. Nothing.

The rumbling sound from the cave rolled toward us again, this time louder than before. I gripped the walking stick firmly, though without the ability to use the eyes, it wasn't a very formidable weapon.

The dismounted guard unfurled a decree and began to read it: "*For crimes against the kingdom and for treason against his lordship, Baron Dorjan, you are hereby sentenced to death.*" He rolled the decree back up. "I have the authority to burn this scroll if you return to the baron with us. He offers you either a full pardon or death. You choose. This will be your only chance to accept his generous offer."

"We haven't committed any crimes against your baron or his kingdom," I called.

"No prince takes it lightly when one of his subjects betrays him."

"We haven't betrayed anyone."

With that, the whiny guard lost his patience. "Who has protected Abaddon from marauding tribes for a thousand years? Who provided a comfortable and safe home for you and your families? Yet now you have dared turn traitor to leave him and serve another? That is your crime!"

"And besides," his partner added, "you've already betrayed your new lord."

"How?"

"We need to get out of here," Leira urged me. "The longer

you talk to them, the more chance their friends will—"

"On your way to the inn," the brusque guard shouted, "you spoke with our friend Namir—who I'm sorry to say is no longer with us. The baron didn't find it amusing when he failed to bring you to the—"

"Tied him hand and foot and fed him alive to the wolfhounds so they wouldn't miss their evening meal," his friend interjected.

Well, that was one less archer to worry about.

The gruff one grunted, then continued, "You also forgot the shepherd's instructions, questioned your direction, considered turning back, and have been careless with the gifts that were given to you."

I had no idea how this man could know all the secret mistakes of my journey, but I was in no mood to ask him. Then I remembered our pardons from the king. "Yes," I yelled, "all those things are true, but we've been pardoned for everything. You have no right to threaten us and no authority over—"

"All authority is ours from Baron Dorjan!" the angry guard cried. "And so, you refuse his offer. Here your treacherous journey ends. Here we will spill your souls!"

The raspy laughter of his friend echoed through the gorge, growing higher and sharper until it became a screech that disappeared into notes no human ears could hear. I expected to see a pack of dogs leap over the cliff and land on us, but no dogs came.

"Kadin," Leira screamed. "Look out!"

An arrow sliced past me and stuck fast into a nearby log.

I took her hand and darted forward.

Another arrow whizzed by. Then I noticed something sticking half-out of the mud.

"Here," I yelled. "A shield!"

I pried it loose from the ground. It must have belonged to some unfortunate vagabond who'd happened too close to this cave some time ago.

It didn't have any straps, but by grasping the edges I could hold it above my head to deflect the arrows. My fingers would be exposed, but that was better than my head or my heart.

When I lifted it, I found that, whatever the shield was made out of, it was remarkably lightweight. I just hoped it was strong enough to stop an arrow.

Leira and I ducked beneath it the best we could. The two men high above us were laughing as they notched fresh arrows . . . laughing as they let them fly . . . laughing as the arrows sank into the earth all around us or bounced off the shield.

"Come on," I said to Leira. "They can't get us in the cave."

Using the shield for protection, we scrambled toward the gaping mouth of the cavern until at last we were out of the archers' range. As I set down the shield, Leira gulped.

"What is it?"

"This isn't a shield," she whispered.

I peered at the shield more closely. "Of course it is, you can—"

"It's a scale."

With slowly sinking horror I realized Leira was right. I'd been holding a large, leathery scale over three feet wide and more than two inches thick at the center, stiff and nearly impenetrable. Four arrows had managed to lodge into it, though none had been able to pierce all the way through. "What kind of animal has scales this big?" I asked, although I had a feeling I already knew the answer.

"I can think of only one."

"Me too," I told her.

Just ahead of us, in the cave, something stirred.

CHAPTER NINE

Apollyon

The sharp smell of sulfur met us at the cave's entrance.

For a few moments, Leira and I stood below the upper lip of the cavern, protected from the archers but not yet ready to venture further into the cave. The river seeped slowly around our feet.

Above us, the cave's opening stretched up at least a hundred feet into the mountainside. Water from massive stalactites dripped all around us. Carefully, I searched the mouth of the cave for any kind of weapon that might have been left behind from one of the unfortunate travelers whose bones littered the entrance. No swords. No daggers. No shields. Nothing.

"Kadin?" Leira said softly.

"Yes?"

"I don't want to go in there."

"That makes two of us."

I heard a branch break, and one of the archers on the pass cursed loudly. After what happened to Namir when he returned empty-handed, I guessed these two wouldn't leave until they knew for certain we were dead. They might be setting up camp or even try climbing down to come after us.

"Maybe we can find another way out of here," Leira offered.

"If we go back out there, we'll be shot."

"But if we stay here . . ." She let her voice trail off as she eyed a pile of charred bones nearby.

I put my hand on her arm and could feel it trembling. "We've come this far. We're going to make it."

"How do you know?"

Good question.

"I guess I just believe that somehow things are going to work out."

She looked at me oddly. "You believe they will."

"Yes." I'm not sure how much of it was hope and how much of it was faith, but I grabbed a bone laying nearby that had a long swathe of tattered fabric still clinging to it. She grimaced as I tied the fabric around the end of the bone and lit it to make a torch.

"That's disgusting."

I held it high. "Come on."

She grabbed the scale we'd been using as a shield, and I led the way into the cave, staff in one hand and torch in the other.

Eerily grinning skulls greeted us from the shallow riverbed. Scores of charred and splintered bones lay submerged at our feet. Some looked like they'd been bitten in half.

Still no sign of the cave's inhabitant.

I wondered how many people—if any—had made it through this cave to the other side of the mountain.

Deliverance—

Or death.

Because the opening to the cave was so large, daylight accompanied us for quite a ways. The main cavern appeared to have one central passageway that slowly descended into the heart of the mountain, a network of smaller tunnels fingered off to the sides. Thirty feet above us on the cave walls, more passageways mouthed open, leading to what I could only imagine was a maze of tunnels winding through the mountain.

We stayed near the walls to avoid being seen by the creature that lived here. As we proceeded, I noticed primitive drawings on the cave walls, perhaps from a band of hunters who'd lived here in the distant past.

Some of the drawings showed people shooting arrows at magnificent animals that I'd never seen before. Others pictured white fluttering figures that might have been faeries—or maybe even angels—intermingling with the people. The final set of drawings showed jagged, frightening forms rising from the earth—and pictures of people being torn apart by something large and dark.

Leira gulped when she saw the drawing. "Kadin?"

"Yes?"

She kept her voice low and guarded. "If the archers' arrows couldn't even pierce through that scale, how are we ever going to fight this thing with nothing more than a hairpin and a walking stick?"

A very good question.

"I'm working on that."

Once we were about a hundred paces into the cave, the sunlight from outside began to dissipate—a little further and our only light came from the makeshift torch. It was starting to burn out but still managed to throw wild, slanting shadows across the cave walls revealing spectacular formations—towering stalagmites surrounding us and the tips of great stalactites looming down from unseen heights above.

Part of the river had channeled underground, but the rest of it pooled around us, rippling out in every direction whenever we took a step.

The tunnel bent slightly in front of us, and as we rounded the corner, Leira whispered, "Have you come up with anything yet?"

"I'm still working on it."

"You'd better hurry."

Less than forty paces in front of us lay the creature.

It was the size of a house and completely covered with dark, interlocking scales. The dragon looked a bit like the lizards I'd seen in the plains near Abaddon when I was growing up, except for his enormous size and two leathery wings unfolding from his sides. His head was shaped like that of a venomous snake and rested on the end of a long serpentine neck. Puffs of smoke spiraled from his nostrils as he breathed.

"Apollyon," I muttered. "I read of him in the book."

We eased quietly behind a boulder.

Leira nodded. "Alcion spoke of this."

The Book of Blood told of an ancient and fiendish creature that had terrorized villages centuries ago. Then, about the time the prince came from the land of the kings, Apollyon had disappeared somewhere in the hills. Over the years, the sightings had become more and more infrequent—or at least the survivors of the sightings had. Now it was clear that the creature had made its home here, on the pathway leading to Celestia, finding a ready source of meat by feeding on unwary vagabonds traveling to the prince's homeland.

The beast was even more terrifying than I'd imagined. But I didn't say that to Leira. "He doesn't look that tough," I whispered.

"You're a terrible liar."

Nearby, deep crevices opened in the cave walls, and bulbous columns of smoke curled upward. Along the edges of the cave, where the river didn't flow, lava bubbled and burst through the skin of the earth, creating weird, fiery reflections on the rippling water around us. Not only was the dragon fire-breathing, so, it seemed, was his lair.

"It's a cave of death," Leira said quietly.

"Or deliverance." I looked around. "We just have to find out how to get delivered."

Our torch flickered weakly.

As I studied the cave, it was immediately clear to me that we needed to get to a safer position. Ahead of us, on the other side of the cavern, I spied a series of tunnels that appeared too small for the dragon to enter. "There." I pointed.

"How do we get there?"

"We go slowly. We go quietly." I kept my voice low. "We do whatever we can, not to attract attention."

A nod.

I looked at the dying torch. "I guess we don't need to give Apollyon a guided tour to his meal." To put it out, I tossed it into the river, but it clattered loudly against a rock before sizzling out.

Oh. Not good.

With a snort of fire, the dragon turned, directing his blazing eyes in our direction. In the wavering light of the lava I could see thick muscles ripple beneath the beast's impenetrable skin. Huge teeth, each the size of my forearm, protruded from his mouth.

Leira gasped.

The dragon let out a puff of rotten-smelling smoke and rose to his feet.

It had seen us.

"Run!" I called.

Leaving the meager protection of the boulder, we dashed toward the smaller caves on the other side of the central cavern, about fifty or sixty paces away.

The dragon roared to life and started toward us.

Though we were running as fast as we could, the closer we came to the center of the tunnel, the deeper the water became, until it reached nearly to my waist. It was impossible to move quickly, but we splashed our way toward the far wall.

Halfway there.

Thunderous splashes told me the dragon was closing.

"Hurry!" I cried, rushing into the darkness, plowing through the water. Then I heard a gasp and a swish of water not far behind me.

"Leira!" I turned.

Based on the ripples, it looked like she'd tripped and fallen about five paces behind me. I started toward the place she'd gone under.

She rose, gulped in a breath.

In the light thrown up by the bubbling lava along the edges of the cavern, I could see the dragon leap off a boulder and land with a tremendous splash beside her. She stumbled backward as he snorted out a cloud of hideous smoke and leaned forward.

"No!" I cried. The beast looked at me and then back at her.

She was slowly backing away from him, holding the shield up for protection.

Apollyon growled.

Do something.

Distract it!

Now!

I threw off my pack and rushed toward the beast, waving my walking stick. Apollyon looked at me momentarily but seemed more interested in Leira and curled his long neck toward her.

I smacked the stick against the thick leathery scales of the dragon's leg, but the creature didn't even seem to notice. He reared back his head like a serpent ready to strike, took a deep breath, and let loose a fiery roar toward Leira.

"Get down!" I yelled.

She had already raised the scale, and the flames licked all around her but didn't reach her.

Apollyon turned to me and drew his head back again.

I gulped in a breath of air and dropped into the water. A moment later I could see the flames glancing off the river's surface above me. The water became ferociously hot, but I managed to wait until the flames had burned out before rising to grab another breath. "Leira!"

"I'm over here . . . here . . . here . . . here . . ." Her voice echoed through the cave, making it impossible to tell where she actually was. But the sound caught the dragon's attention, and he lifted into the air with his huge wings. For a creature that size, he was unbelievably quick.

"Where are you? . . . you . . . you . . . ?" I yelled.

"Over here . . . here . . ."

I scanned the cave and saw a glint of light reflect off the scale. She'd wedged herself into a small opening on the other side of the cavern, perhaps forty paces away. It wasn't the tunnel we'd been aiming for, but it looked like it would at least offer her some protection. My eyes were becoming accustomed to the dim light of the cave by then, and I could see the dragon winging its way high into the mountain where it rested on a ledge about sixty feet above Leira.

"Don't come out," I called. "He's waiting for you." The words were distorted by the echoing chamber, but I was confident that at least she'd caught my meaning.

Keeping an eye on the dragon, I hurried back to the place where I'd dropped my pack, found it floating in the water, and carried it, as well as my walking stick, toward the tunnels we'd been hoping to get to.

I stowed the walking stick against the cave wall and tried stuffing my pack between two boulders to get it out of the water, but the corner of the Book of Blood caught on the edge of a rock. Rather than pound it in and risk damaging the book, I opened the pack and reached in to reposition it. As I did, I smelled something other than death and sulfur. Flowers? Perfume? Odd. It reminded me of the dream I'd had at the beginning of my journey—the fragrance of lilies.

Groping for the Book of Blood, I found that it wasn't there. Instead, I wrapped my fingers around the thing that rested in its place. Pulled out my hand.

In it I held a cross-shaped, double-edged hand axe.

A burst of fire slithered up the cave wall, illuminating the passageway, and I saw that Leira had leaned out of her hiding place. She gasped. "Where did you get that?" From where she was now, the echo was fainter and her words, clearer.

"The book turned into it," I shouted.

"Magik." I heard the quiet echo of the word meander through the chamber: " . . . magik . . . magik . . ."

"I guess so," I said to myself.

The shepherd had told me about this land being powerful, a place where both good and evil come to life. Maybe this axe was the good. Maybe some force of magik from the book was reaching out to deliver us from this beast.

Deliverance.

Or death.

But how was I supposed to fight a dragon with a hand axe that probably wouldn't even put a dent into one of its scales?

I looked around the cave. Stalagmites rose from the floor and, near where the dragon was lurking, several huge stalactites hung from the ceiling.

Come on . . . come on . . . there's got to be some way to . . .

I examined the cave floor and then glanced at the ceiling again and I had an idea. It seemed preposterous, but I figured at this point anything was worth a try.

Grasping the axe, I made my way toward the cave's wall.

Leira peered out of her hiding place. "Where are you going?"

"I've got an idea."

"What do you want me to do?"

"Stay alive."

I stuck the handle of the axe into the back of my belt and began to climb the slimy walls of the cave, using outcroppings for hand holds and foot holds.

This is crazy. It's never going to work!

And then another voice, not audible, but still, somehow present: *Trust me. It'll work. Just trust me.*

While I was trying to figure out whose voice it might be, one of my handholds pulled loose. My hand and one leg swung from the rock face, but thankfully I was able to keep my other on the ledge below me and hold on with my left hand. The rock that had come loose—a boulder bigger than my head—flew away from the wall and splashed into the water far below me. Heart hammering, I thought for sure the dragon would fly over and snatch me from the cave wall with his huge talons. But he didn't. Now unsure of every handhold, every foothold, I climbed.

At last I reached the second level of the cave. A tunnel sloped gently up toward the ceiling of the main—

A splash.

I jerked my head around and saw that the dragon had left

his perch and was beginning to search for Leira, sniffing at the walls and poking his head into small passageways.

Hurry, Kadin.

Go!

Using the light from his intermittent blasts of fire to guide me, I entered the ascending tunnel and saw that it wove upward and ended in the ceiling of the cave.

Far below me, near where Leira was hiding, the dragon poked its head into a crevice and snapped its jaws at something in the darkness.

Do it. Now!

Carefully, I laid on my back and wedged my feet in place, hoping I would be able to lean out far enough and reach what I'd climbed up here for. I positioned myself, maneuvered the axe handle out of my belt with my right hand, and found a crack in the ceiling that I could grab with my left hand to help hold myself in place.

Then I faced the thing I was about to chop through.

The stalactite hung just a few feet away from my face. It was at least twelve feet long and must have weighed a couple of tons. I drew back my arm and with all the strength I could muster at this strange angle, I swung the axe at the base of the stalactite where it was attached to the ceiling.

The blade connected with the stone with a sharp *clang* that caught the attention of Apollyon, just as I'd hoped it would. The beast snapped his head in my direction and, with amazing agility, turned in one fluid motion to face me.

I swung the axe against the stalactite again. *Clang!*

The dragon raised its wings and flapped into the air.

Please work. Come on. Come on!

I had no good reason to think that the axe that'd appeared in my pack would be able to cut through solid stone. And yet . . . a feeling, an inkling, an idea I couldn't define but that had somehow formed in my mind, prodded me forward. Told me to try again.

Using the axe that had been a book, I chopped at the stalactite again and again as the dragon flew toward me.

And again.

But the stalactite did not crack. Did not fall.

The dragon landed on a ledge below me. Holding on with his talons, he clung to the cave wall, faced me, and I had a feeling I knew what was coming. I ducked back into the crevice, pulling my coat over my face as the dragon spewed fire directly at me.

The flames engulfed me, filling the narrow tunnel I was wedged into. I could feel the heat licking at my face, singeing my hair. I might've been killed instantly, but the coat Reyhan had given me seemed to give supernatural protection from the flames.

I knew the dragon would need a moment to inhale again before his next blast. I edged out of the opening to try again with the axe, but saw Apollyon rearing back his head. He was about thirty or forty feet away, directly below me, and had his wings outstretched like a giant bat.

I didn't have enough time to swing the axe, only enough time to slide back into the passage where I'd wedged my legs. Once again flames curled around me. Despite the protection of the coat, the rocks surrounding me were absorbing the heat of the flames. If I didn't do something quickly, the beast was going to cook me alive.

As soon as the flames dissipated, I leaned my head and torso out of the opening again, flung back my right arm, and struck the stalactite with the fiercest blow I could muster. The force of the impact jarred my body loose, causing me to slip from the enclosure, leaving me hanging by my left arm, swinging from the roof of the cave.

I dropped the axe, which was of no more use to me now, and frantically searched the ceiling with my right hand for something to hold onto. *Come on. Come on!*

Nothing.

My left hand was slipping—

Hurry! Something, anything!

I brushed my hand across—

There!

A crack!

I jammed the fingers of my right hand into a narrow slit in the rock and looked down, only to see the dragon rushing toward me.

It hadn't worked. I'd failed.

But then I heard a faint cracking sound. I craned my neck and saw a thin crack crawling across the base of the stalactite.

Then the crack widened as the weight of the formation pulled the giant stone dagger free from the roof of the cave.

And, in a graceful, effortless dive, the stalactite broke free and plummeted toward the cave floor. It fell at a slight angle as the weight of the upper portion tried to find the ground first, but before it could spin, it found its mark.

Apollyon was directly under the stalactite as it fell. Like a two-ton sword, the formation stabbed into Apollyon's back with crushing strength. They plunged together, and crashed to the ground where the stalactite buried itself deep into the creature's body, pinning him to the muddy floor of the cave.

The dragon sent out a tremendous screech that shook the cavern and seemed to echo forever.

As I tried to swing my legs into the opening in the rock, he snapped his long neck back and forth, frantically—even smacking his head into the wall of the cave. He tried to flap his wings and be free of the huge stone impaling him, but the stalactite had fallen with impossible accuracy. Based on the amount of dark blood spraying from the dragon's wounds, it must certainly have pierced the beast's heart.

Hearing the cries, Leira stepped out of her hiding place.

"No," I cried. "Get back!"

But my warning was too late

The dying dragon's eyes locked onto her and his clawed

foot shot out and grabbed her, wrapping tightly around her waist.

"I'm coming!" I finally managed to get one leg and then the other into the tunnel so I could work my way back down to the ground.

Leira screamed as the beast pulled her off her feet and dragged her toward his mouth.

For a moment I considered jumping to get to her, but the fall of more than eighty feet onto the rocky riverbed would almost certainly kill me.

I scrambled down the tunnel, losing sight of Leira momentarily, but I could still hear her cries for help echo through the cave.

Please, please, no!

The access tunnel ended.

"I'm coming!" I still needed to climb down nearly forty feet of cave wall. But I could see I would never make it to her in time.

The beast had managed to drag her nearly all the way to his mouth. At the last instant Leira threw something at the face of the dragon. He shrieked and flung her into the darkness, clawing desperately at his face.

Leira landed in the water with a splash.

"Leira!" I was downclimbing toward a ledge twelve feet below me.

Nothing.

"Leira!"

A moment later: "I'm okay!"

Apollyon writhed against the grip of death, but at last, dropped into a quivering heap. Even from where I was, thirty feet above the ground, I could see dark blood gush from his mouth and flow into a widening circle that pooled into the water flowing lazily around his body.

Leira looked my way. "How did you do that? With the stalactite?"

"I don't know."

I eased my way foothold by foothold, handhold by handhold, down the wet rocks.

"You killed a dragon," she said admiringly.

"*We* killed it." I was only twenty feet from the cave's floor. "What did you throw in its face?"

"Healing water. I was pouring some on the burns on my arms when it grabbed me."

"I guess it doesn't heal dragons."

"I guess not," she said, then added, "We only have half a flask left."

"Let's hope we just met our last dragon."

I was about fifteen feet from the floor of the cave when my foot slipped. I cried out as I fell awkwardly into the darkness and landed *kerplunk!* in waist-deep water.

Leira hurried toward me. "Kadin! Are you all right?"

I stood and patted myself down, making sure there were no broken bones. "Yeah." I let out a sigh of relief. "Well, at least we're out of danger for awhile."

"Not quite." She was staring grimly past me. "We still have to find our way through this cave."

CHAPTER TEN

Voices

After we'd cleaned up a bit with the water from the section of the river that was not filling with the black blood of the dragon, we took a few minutes to get our bearings.

The healing water had burned away the leathery skin of the dragon's face, revealing part of his jaw and the roots of his great teeth. Leira took the axe and chopped at one of them, wrenching it free from his mouth.

"What's that for?"

She slid the foot-long fang into her pack. "Keepsake."

As soon as she set down the axe, the handle began to swell, then widen and expand, forming into the shape of a book again. The blade sank into the pages, and the wooden exterior transformed before our eyes and turned into soft, supple leather.

"It's a good thing that didn't happen five minutes ago," I said.

"I still can't believe you killed that thing," she said.

"The stalactite did all the heavy work."

"It didn't fall on its own." Using light from the lava bubbling from a fissure in the wall to help us, she consulted the book. "It looks like we'll have to climb a sheer rock face to an outpost when we reach the far end of the cave."

"Figures." I looked at the sloping passageway ahead of us. "At least it's all downhill until then."

As we proceeded forward, the main corridor eventually narrowed, and the trail snaked its way along the edge of the river, part of which reemerged on our right. On our left, the ground dropped away into nothingness. We tossed some rocks over the edge and waited for them to land but never heard them hit the bottom.

"Don't slip," I said.

"Don't worry," Leira replied.

With no torch of any kind and fewer fissures spitting up lava beside us now, the cave became oppressively dark. The darkness seemed stifling, suffocating even, as if it were trying to swallow us along with the light. Rather than the sharp smell of sulfur, the air here was damp and pungent. It reminded me of the smell of an open grave.

Which didn't exactly encourage me.

Progress was frustratingly slow. I wondered if maybe the book would change into something else to help us. A torch maybe. Or a flying carpet to get us out of here fast. I decided to try.

I slipped off my pack and slid my hand inside. Nope. Just a book.

Leira waited for me to put my pack back on. "Poor Castel and Biminak."

During our encounter with the dragon, I'd almost forgotten about them. "They didn't deserve what happened to them."

"No, they didn't."

It was blatantly obvious, but I felt like the words bore saying, "We have to be careful."

We felt our way along the edge of the trail for a few minutes and then saw two bobbing lights far ahead of us.

"Do you think it might be the archers?" There was more than just a hint of fear in her voice.

"I doubt it. How could they have gotten ahead of us?"

"Whoever it is, they're coming our way."

She was right. They were coming our way—fast. How they could move so quickly along the narrow pathway and still keep their footing was a mystery to me. Fearing they might not be friendly, I wished I had the axe again. I didn't know how I could possibly do battle with anyone in these tight quarters with only a book. I grabbed the staff with both hands. Raised it high.

"Please tell me they're vagabonds," Leira muttered.

Somewhat hesitantly, I called to them, "Vagabonds?"

"Get out of our way," one of them yelled. It was a woman's voice, shrill and desperate. The good thing was, she didn't sound like she was about to attack us. The bad thing was, she sounded like she was running for her life.

"What is it?" Leira cried. "What's wrong?"

The two lights didn't slow down, and the closer they came the more I realized it would be tricky getting past them. "Slow down a minute," I called. "Are you vagabonds?"

"Yes," came the reply. A man this time. "Get out of our way!"

They were just a dozen paces away and still running.

"Stop running!" Leira warned, "or you'll knock us all into the pit!"

That seemed to calm them a bit. The torchbearers began to walk, albeit quickly.

I repositioned myself as far to the side as I dared. "What are you running from?"

The woman, who was in front, spoke up first. "Up ahead." She was out of breath. "Voices . . ." The two of them were close enough now for me to see their faces and the small scars on their necks where they'd been healed.

"What kind of voices?"

"From the pit," the man responded. He was rugged looking with a full beard and broad shoulders. His partner appeared petite but sinewy and tough from many days on the trail. "They came at us from everywhere. We'd rather face the dragon than—"

"The dragon is dead," Leira said. "Kadin killed it." I heard a note of pride in her voice.

"Both of us did," I corrected. "Together."

The two vagabonds stopped, stared at me. "Are you a wizard?"

I shook my head. "No. Something extraordinary happened. I can't explain it."

We told them about the axe, and the man nodded. "Kiral, the King."

I didn't know what the axe had to do with King Kiral, but that seemed to settle the matter in their minds, so I left it at that. Though they were still anxious to get out of the cave, we talked for a few minutes. They seemed to be more knowledgeable about King Kiral and his ways than we were. That frightened me a little, because as much as they knew, as far as they'd come, they were still ready to turn back.

They told us they'd managed to slip past the dragon while he was out hunting. They'd waited for three days for him to leave the cave and then hurried in before he could return. As they spoke, the two of them kept looking over their shoulders and pressing us to go back with them to the gorge.

"If the dragon is dead, there's no question about it," the woman said. "It's better to go back. Come with us, we'll—"

"No," I told her. "We're pressing on to Celestia. Besides, there are two archers back there waiting for us."

"We can handle two archers," the man said.

"Maybe," I said. "Maybe not." I tried one more time to dissuade our two new friends from turning back. "Listen, let's all travel together. Four people have a better chance of making it than just two. Besides, we have to get through this cave to get to Celestia. The voices can't be that bad."

But it was no use. Their minds were made up. No matter how hard Leira and I tried, we couldn't convince them. Something up ahead in the cave had scared them enough to make them turn back after all those weeks of traveling.

At last, they eased passed us.

"The strength of Kiral be with you," the man said.

I'd never heard that salutation before. I wasn't sure what to say. "Yes . . . and with—"

"With you as well," he explained.

"With you as well," I said.

The woman, who'd been avoiding looking at me, finally met my gaze. "Take this." She handed me her torch. "You'll need it." They still had the man's torch, so I gladly accepted hers.

"Thank you."

And with that, they were gone. For a little while I heard their voices echoing through the darkness, but eventually they were swallowed up by the sound of rustling water near our feet.

"Voices?" Leira said. "They turned back because of voices? What kind of voices could they be?"

"I was wondering the same thing. Let's go. But stay close."

The farther we went, the more the darkness seemed to engulf the sound of the river, making the pathway eerily soundless. Still, we knew it was there—and on our other side was the pit. We walked that narrow escarpment for what seemed like miles.

At times I saw glimmers of white flutter near my head, as if something were escaping through the thick darkness. I thought of the cave drawings we'd seen earlier and wondered if these were faeries or angels who would guide us along the path. I could almost make out the wings, but not quite. I reached out to touch one of them, and it flitted away.

And that's when the voices started.

Moans. Screams. Helpless wails. Rising and echoing, surrounding us—howls of souls in deep agony pierced the living darkness.

Leira edged closer to me. "Do you think it's the voices of those who've fallen into the pit?" She had to yell just to be heard.

"Maybe," I called back. The voices rose to a deafening roar of madness. I thought of the man and woman who'd hurried past us. *No wonder they turned back.*

Leira drew herself up to my ear. "It kind of sounds like the baron's dungeon." And with that grim thought on our minds, we pressed on.

In here, the light of our torch faded after only a few feet. On the edge of the torchlight we began to see flickers of faces slicing through the darkness. Horrible, ghost-like apparitions curling on the edge of what was real and what was not.

Not faeries.

Definitely not angels.

It was as if the curtain between this world and the next were thinner here in the oppressive darkness of this vile cave. All around us I could feel another world unfolding, trying to spread its dark wings—a world of mists and wraiths and demons, stained with terror and shame.

Faces filled with terrible teeth and bulging eyes stretched against the curtain of the real, trying to come through, to break free. Lips curled back, teeth bared. Sometimes I heard the rattle of chains scraping against the rocks. Other times, the sharp click of talons and claws filled the air. Dark creatures were lurking on the border of darkness just beyond our light, living on the screams of the dead, thriving on the despair of the lost.

At times, I thought I might be asleep, dreaming the final nightmare. But then Leira would brush against me, and I'd be jarred back to reality. Only the flicker of light seemed to keep the nightmarish forms at bay. That torch. That glorious, wondrous torch handed to us by a vagabond who had been too terrified to keep going.

"If we ever get out of this alive," I said to Leira in a moment when the wailing seemed to die down, "I'm never taking daylight for granted again."

"Or silence," she said.

The farther we walked, the hungrier the darkness seemed. Tendrils of it wandered into the light of our torch, then sizzled angrily as they died out. Living shadows were reaching into the light and trying to grab us.

I began to see things I knew couldn't possibly be there. Once, I thought I saw a giant bird ahead of us, materializing in midair, growing from the shadows that seeped from the cave. All I could think of was that it appeared to be the color of death. It settled in our pathway, stretching its wings across the trail. Maybe it was the soul of the slain dragon, reappearing to seek vengeance on me.

It's not real, I told myself over and over as we neared it. I knew that whatever happened we had to keep going. We had to keep walking if we were ever going to make it to Celestia. At last the vision receded into the blackness and disappeared.

Then I heard a voice as clear as day, *You'll never get out of this alive.*

I turned to Leira. "Did you say something?"

"No. Why?"

"I thought I heard you."

"It wasn't me."

After a few minutes, the voice returned. I couldn't tell if it was coming from ahead of us or beside us or from somewhere inside my head. *You should have turned back with those other two. They made it farther than you ever will. With their help you could have gotten past the archers. Now look at you.*

"No," I blurted. "We can make it."

Leira looked at me oddly, then gazed ahead of us.

Slowly, we proceeded forward.

In the strangely echoing chamber, mixed with the sounds of gurgling water and vacant screams, alone with my thoughts, I couldn't tell what I was thinking or what I was saying anymore, or which words might have come from the gruesome faces hovering on the brink of the darkness, whispering thoughts to my soul.

It's not too late. You have family back there in the valley. People who care about you. A life! And what have you chosen instead? You were almost drowned in a swamp, killed by archers, eaten by a dragon—and this is supposed to be the way to freedom and—

"Stop it!" I yelled.

"What are you talking about?" Leira said. "Why are you yelling at me?"

"It's not you." I was shaken. Jarred. But I tried to downplay my fear. "It's nothing. I'm fine. Never mind."

Obviously, Leira wasn't hearing the same voices I was.

I tried to shake off the doubts, but once they started, they came like a rockslide, one evil thought setting loose an avalanche of others, and they all came crashing down on me at the same time. Things I hated myself for even considering crept into my mind. *You like her, don't you? You wish you could do to her what the guards did in the dungeon. All to—*

"No!"

"Kadin." Leira placed her hand on my arm. "Are you okay?"

I was so upset by then that I was struggling for breath. *Oh, please!* cried the true voice of my soul, *Giver of Dreams, take away these nightmares!*

"Leira," I said at last. "Let me hold your hand."

"Why?"

"I need to know what's real."

And so we walked along that precipice hand in hand amidst the screams and whispers of murmuring ghosts that tried to lure us closer to the edge of the pit. I could see why the other two vagabonds had turned back. If I'd been alone, I probably would have done the same.

Hunger, thirst, the need for rest—they all seemed like memories of another world rather than things I would ever experience again. There was no way to tell how long we walked, but finally, after what seemed like months of walking—but what must have only been a few hours—I saw the distant glow of sunlight filtering into the cave.

"Yes!" I cried. We hurried forward as fast as we dared. "We're almost there."

But as we neared the end of the passageway, I didn't see any vegetation outside the cave. Just space.

Emptiness.

Curious, I led Leira toward it.

The temperature all through the cavern had been cool, but near the exit the air became brisk. Icy. We began to see our breath as we huffed our way toward the cave's opening, where ice crystals had crept in and buried the boulders in thick, bristly frost.

Beside us, the river reappeared, emerging from its underground channel with renewed fury and purpose, roiling and churning not far from our feet.

The pit on our left had disappeared, and we edged along the cave wall to avoid the tug of the water, which rushed past us and disappeared into nothingness at the cave's opening.

With each step, the dissipating darkness muffled less noise from the river. The water's roar became deafening, making discussion nearly impossible.

"We're almost there!" I shouted.

"But where?" Leira replied.

We arrived at the cave's exit.

We'd been walking downhill since we entered the cave, so I expected we would be near the floor of the valley on this side of the mountain range, but instead, the cave opened near the summit of a towering peak. The river cascading from the cave shot out over empty space, plummeting into a frozen valley thousands of feet below us. The river was rushing too fast to freeze, but in the bitterly cold air, the spray along the edges of the waterfall had frozen against the face of the cliff.

I stared across the sweeping expanse to the snow-covered peaks that rose against the far horizon. "Unbelievable," I breathed.

How was this possible? How could we be higher now than we'd been when we left the archers? *It's like we've entered another world.*

As I stared at the distant mountains, the valley, which had been glistening in the sunlight, dimmed beneath the shadow of a huge bank of clouds that slid across the sun.

A thin ledge, barely wide enough to stand on, led up the side of the rock face toward the mountain's peak. Could that really be our trail? It had to be. There was no other possibility.

I touched Leira's elbow and pointed to the icy lip of rock. She nodded and followed me.

Frigid wind bit into our faces as we left the cave and edged up the trail toward the summit. It was less than a thousand paces, but it took us several hours as we plodded slowly along the ice-encrusted trail.

Though we were tired, we dared not rest for long, fearing that the wind might sweep us off the cliff and into the empty air behind us.

Thankfully, as we neared the top of the mountain, the roar of the river was less deafening, and Leira pointed to a castle about a mile away on the top of a neighboring ridge. "That's it," she said. "The king's outpost."

We made our way toward it, but the thick clouds now covering the sky let loose a flurry of blinding snow. The blizzard moved toward us with astonishing speed and soon engulfed the trail, making it impossible to see more than a few feet. I hoped we were still heading in the right direction, but there was no way to tell for sure.

We trudged along, with leggings pulled over our hands to keep our fingers from freezing. Autumn had obviously passed into winter while we were walking through the cave. I couldn't help but wonder how long our journey through that tunnel had actually taken.

The clothes Reyhan had given us served well to protect us from the weather, but even they wouldn't be able to keep us warm forever. We had to make it to that outpost.

We turned our collars against the biting wind and moved slowly through the deepening snow.

Both of us were exhausted from the descent into the gorge, the encounter with the baron's archers, the attack of Apollyon, and the long trip through the howling darkness. Now, with the blizzard encircling us, it was almost enough to make me want to give up.

We stumbled on as far as we could, but finally, unable to take another step, I collapsed onto the snow. Somewhere ahead of us was the castle—I knew that. And Leira was close behind me. I turned back only to see her drop to the ground as well.

"Leira," I called weakly.

She lay still.

I tried to crawl to her but never made it. The last thing I remember before passing out was seeing a large figure, a man the size of a bear, ambling toward me with unblinking eyes as white as the swirling snow.

CHAPTER ELEVEN

Reunion

I blinked my eyes open.

No longer was I in a snowbank, but in a room on a soft bed. Warm, gentle light surrounded me. I thought I heard the howl of wind, and I guessed it was probably the blizzard outside, but I couldn't be sure. I was tired, so tired. Warmth surrounded me, embraced me, and I closed my eyes again.

I dreamt and slept and dreamt again. Occasionally I would awaken to the sound of the screaming wind as the storm grew more intense. Once, as I looked around the room, I wondered if everything had been a dream, if maybe even now I was dreaming that I was awake. Time swirled past me with the snow.

Then I heard a knock on the door and a voice that didn't seem like a dream at all. "Kadin?"

"Leira?" I sat up wearily. "Is that you?"

She propped open my door. "How are you?" She sounded concerned. A thin outline of light surrounded her.

I still wasn't sure she was real. "Are you a dream?"

"Why, were you dreaming about me?" Backlit as she was, I couldn't see her face, but there was a touch of a smile in her voice.

"Um." I was still having difficulty thinking clearly. "This may sound like a strange question, but are we dead?"

"Not the last time I checked. But I was starting to worry about you. It's time to get up. It's almost noon."

"Noon?" I groaned.

I always awoke with the sun while we were on the trail, but it seemed like every time I found a nice, comfortable bed, I ended up sleeping half the day. Finally, I rubbed my head. "Yeah . . . okay. Wow, was I tired."

"I know. I'll see you in the commons. It's easy to find. Just follow the hall. There's someone here who wants to see you."

Then the door closed.

I flopped down again, yawned, and stretched my arms. I was here, really here, in this castle on top of this mountain within these windswept peaks. But who would want to see me here? Maybe the lord of the castle? The person I'd seen approaching me in the storm? Probably one of the two.

After a few minutes, I got up, splashed some water on my face from a small fountain in the corner of the room, and made my way down a long hallway. I could hear people laughing somewhere ahead of me.

Despite the blizzard outside, the corridor was surprisingly warm, more like a womb than a stone hallway. Light seeped from thin cracks in the wall, both heating and illuminating the passageway with a dreamy, ethereal brightness. Amazingly, no wind found its way through the cracks. Paintings of men, women, and children lined the walls. Sometimes entire families were pictured together, although I didn't recognize any of the people.

I noticed a number of other hallways intersecting the main one. Most of them had no doors, but one corridor contained a door covered with an intricate carving of the same bird that appeared on the head of my walking stick. A phoenix. From beyond the door, I could hear strange, gurgling sounds. Curious, I tried the handle. It was locked.

When I heard more sounds in there, choked and frightened this time, I hurried back to the main hallway.

It ended in a high-ceilinged room that glowed even brighter than the hallways. At first I thought it was magik, that the entire castle was enchanted, but when I looked up, I noticed that the ceiling was inset with long strips of thick glass designed to let sunlight through but keep the weather out. The windows were slanted so snow and ice could easily slide off. Beyond them, winter raged against the castle.

Looking around, I realized that glass filled the cracks between the boulders in the walls. This entire castle was an intricate marvel of stone fitted in glass, designed to spread and disperse light and warmth to even the most secluded hallway. I stared around in wonder. No one in Abaddon could have designed anything like this.

"Kadin," a voice called to me. It sounded somewhat familiar, but I couldn't place it. I scanned the room. Then I saw him, sitting at a table behind a tall mug of ale, the person Leira had told me about.

"Alcion?" I gasped. "Is it you?"

"I hope so; otherwise I have no idea who I might be." He stood and greeted me with a hearty embrace. Leira, who'd been sitting by his side, also rose. Alcion said to me, "We were starting to get worried about you. We thought you might never wake up."

"He's better on the trail," Leira noted. "He likes to sleep in when his bed is comfortable."

"Thanks," I muttered.

Alcion reached for his mug. "Well, it may be winter outside, but at least we've finally stopped hibernating in here. I offer a toast to new beginnings."

I looked around for a mug to return his toast and noticed, for the first time, three beautiful young women standing in the corner of the room, watching me. They looked a few years older than Leira, and at first I thought my eyes were playing tricks on me because their faces were identical. The girls were different in garb only—one was adorned in rich reds, another wore a yellow, lemon-colored dress, and the third, an elegant blue one.

A man nearly twice my size emerged from a doorway near them. He lumbered toward us and thrust a mug into my hand, then turned almost immediately toward Alcion, not leaving me much time to get a good look at his face.

"A toast is not a toast without a drink!" the man announced.

I thanked him and let my cup bump Alcion's and Leira's, which were already raised. The huge man waited for each of us to bump his cup with our own, maybe because if he'd swung his out, it would have shattered our cups. We all had a deep swallow and sat down to enjoy a meal and conversation.

When I looked over my shoulder, the three young women were gone.

◆ ◆ ◆ ◆

"I saw a door with a bird carved into it," I told Alcion as we began to eat. "In one of the other hallways."

"Mmm," he said. "We call it the Door of the Phoenix. Behind it lies the Hall of Tales."

"I heard sounds. I was concerned. I tried the handle, but it was locked."

"That's because you weren't ready for its stories yet." It was the hulking man who'd plopped down in the chair beside me. "When you're ready, the door will let you in."

Alcion gestured toward him. "Kadin, have you met my brother, Gaius, yet?"

The large man nodded. "We met outside."

So, yes, he was the one who'd found me in the snow.

I extended my hand to him. "Pleased to meet you. Thanks for helping me when—" Only then did I notice that Gaius stared straight ahead into space, and that his eyes were strangely glazed over.

He's blind.

"I um . . ." I sputtered. "I didn't know Alcion had a brother." I found Gaius's hand and shook it.

"Not brothers by birth," Gaius said in his deep, growling voice, "brothers by choice."

Alcion leaned close to me. "He always does this, Kadin. Talks in riddles. Considers himself quite clever, I believe." He winked. "Personally, I think he's been living up here too long. Just smile and nod."

"I heard that," Gaius grumbled.

Alcion laughed. "Brother, you may be blind, but you can see more than the rest of us."

"Those who see only with their eyes are the blindest of all," Gaius retorted.

Leira nudged me. "I've been telling them all about our trip."

"Yes, yes," Alcion said. "Congratulations on your fight with Apollyon. Well done!"

"Thanks, but really, it wasn't me. It was magik—"

Suddenly the mood of the room chilled and Gaius's face hardened. Alcion held up his palm in warning. "Be careful saying that word around here. No one up here believes in magik."

Gaius grunted his agreement.

Feeling a little uneasy, I decided to change the subject. "I saw three women over there in the corner a few minutes ago. Are they guests like us, or do they live here?"

"We are all guests," Gaius said, his voice cool. "Some just stay longer than others."

I wondered if that comment was aimed at me for mentioning magik.

"They're sisters," Alcion explained. "Shika, Michi, and Asvina. Shika is the oldest by three minutes, Asvina the youngest by two. They do their best to help us keep them straight by dressing in different colors. Shika prefers red; Michi wears yellow; and Asvina, well, she wears whatever color she feels like that day. They work here, Kadin. Maybe later they can show you around."

"I'd like that."

Leira mumbled under her breath, "I'll bet you would."

"I heard that," I whispered with a smile.

"I wanted you to," she replied.

At one point during the meal, I asked Alcion if he'd been back to Abaddon since I'd left. He shook his head. "No, but I do have some news from there about your friend Erikon."

"Erikon!" I exclaimed. "Is he okay?"

"Well, that's a question only time can answer. Some of my friends who travel and share news, much as I do, tell me he made it back to Abaddon safely. When he arrived though, the people laughed at him and would make no end of calling him names—traitor, turncoat, coward—things of that nature. I believe he's worse off now than if he'd never started the trip in the first place."

Being familiar with Abaddon, I could picture it all happening just as Alcion had described. Before reading the book, I would have treated Erikon the same way. "Any word on my family?"

"No, I'm sorry. But I think I would have heard if they'd become vagabonds."

I nodded quietly. "I see."

We ate in silence for a few minutes, and then Alcion began to ask Leira and me more detailed questions about our journey. As we answered him, Gaius gave us his own interpretation of the events of our trip.

"So, Kadin." Alcion motioned at me with his fork. "How long did it take you to decide to leave Abaddon after we spoke in the alley?"

"A few months," I admitted. "I'm ashamed to say so. But finally I knew I had to leave."

Gaius nodded. He had a mouthful of food, which he quickly swallowed. "Those who love their lives more than their souls will lose both," he said, "but those who love truth will gain all."

Leira and I told them about our trials and difficulties along the way. "The bitter must come before the sweet," Gaius explained. We spoke of our encounter with Castel and Biminak. "People take many shortcuts to deal with guilt," he said. We mentioned the couple who'd turned back in the cave. "Vagabonds cannot be overcome; they can only give in or give up," he offered. "A vagabond is only as strong as he is honest about his—"

"Or her," interrupted Leira.

Gaius cleared his throat slightly. "Yes, or *her* weaknesses."

Alcion took a drink of ale, then set down his cup. "So then, before you faced Apollyon, you had to journey through the gorge."

"Yes," I said. "I hated the idea of descending into a valley after we'd made it that high into the mountains, but it seemed like the only way to move forward."

As I finished my sentence, Leira and I simultaneously turned toward Gaius to await his reply. We weren't disappointed. "Sometimes the pathway to the peak is through the lowest valley," he said. "Those who never descend beyond themselves will never rise above themselves."

I nodded slowly as if I understood, then whispered to Leira, "Do you have any idea what he's talking about?"

"Not a clue," she replied under her breath.

Gaius drummed his fingers on the table. "Those who whisper reveal more about themselves than those who shout."

I sighed, and Leira just shook her head.

Just then, the red-clad Shika, moving as gracefully and quietly as a doe, brought us dessert. Alcion thanked her; she bowed to him, then backed out of the room. As we began to eat our slices of warm, fruity pie, Alcion said, "You could never have journeyed this far without having some questions arise. Anything you've been wondering about? Anything you'd like to ask? Now's your chance with the riddle-speaking, all-seeing Gaius here."

Gaius seemed pleased by the comment.

Leira and I were silent for a moment. I didn't want to admit I'd questioned anything, and I had the feeling the same was true for Leira.

"Where there are no questions," Gaius said, "there is no courage."

"I guess I ought to have a lot of courage then," I said lightly.

"It is one thing to have courage when things are easy," Gaius replied, "and quite another to have courage when things are hard."

He was starting to get on my nerves.

Leira spoke up. "Um, yes, Alcion—or Gaius—either of you can answer if you like. I have a question. Why aren't more rich people and educated people vagabonds? We haven't met too many vagabonds along the way, but from all I've seen and heard, the powerful and influential rarely make the trip to Celestia. Why is that?"

Alcion deferred to his friend. "Gaius?"

"What would you call those on a sinking ship who begin by throwing the most precious cargo overboard first?" he asked Leira.

She thought for a moment. "Well, if it's possible that the ship might be rescued they would be fools. Instead, they should throw away the worthless items first."

A nod. "Yes. Only fools would throw away what is precious and cling to what is worthless. And what would you call those who have gold in their pockets, but no peace in their hearts?"

"I see," Leira said. "Some people are poor even though they appear rich."

Gaius nodded. "In some lands all of life is backward. The liar seems truthful. The madman seems sane. Fools seem wise, and the poor seem rich. In Celestia, all is as it should be."

"But what of those who put off the journey? who say they'll start it someday?" Leira asked. "What about them?"

"Those who say they'll start the journey someday are like those who have a week to run twenty miles to save their lives and wait until the last hour of the final day to start their trip."

After a moment, Alcion turned to me. "What about you, Kadin? What questions do you have?"

I did have a question. That was the thing. But it seemed disrespectful to ask it.

"Go on," Gaius said, sensing my hesitation.

I took a deep breath. "Well, I've been wondering about King Kiral. I know what the book says—that he's kind and gracious and good to those who serve him. But the journey Leira and I have been on seems to tell a different story. We've had nothing but trouble and danger since we left Abaddon. And . . ." I let my voice trail off, trying to figure out how to phrase my question. If I said what I was thinking, I expected Gaius would give me a quick rebuke for being presumptuous or impudent.

"So," Alcion said, guessing at my thoughts, "if the king is good and powerful, why is the life of a vagabond so full of pain?"

"Yes."

"Gaius is more qualified to answer that than I am," Alcion said, "for he has suffered more in his life."

The blind man leaned forward, staring blankly past me. "Pain seems to speak against either the goodness or the power of the king. It is the question at the heart of all questions." Then he said something that surprised me: "And I don't have an answer for you."

If even Gaius doesn't know, maybe there isn't one.

After a brief pause he continued, "I've seen hints of the answer—in the way a doctor must sometimes cause pain in order to heal, in the way a father disciplines his child, in the way a general allows hardship to test the allegiance of his soldiers, in the way a mother gives her son the freedom to leave home, even though he might turn into a thief or a murderer. But these are hints and not answers. In the end you must choose which to trust—your perception of your experiences or the word of the king. I have made my choice."

We were all quiet.

Finally, Alcion broke the silence, "By the end of your journey, Kadin. I think you'll see that the king was doing far more than you ever imagined to help you all along the way."

Gaius concluded, "In this land, in all lands outside of Celestia, you shouldn't expect to walk far without experiencing danger and tears and pain. But there is one who gives rest by his sorrow and life by his death."

Another riddle.

I wasn't sure that answered my question. I wasn't even sure

what it meant, but I thanked them both and went back to my meal. Just as we finished eating, Michi, the yellow-clad sister, arrived. Without a word she bowed before us. Gaius and Alcion returned her bow and somewhat awkwardly, Leira and I followed suit. Then Gaius said, "Michi, please show our friends around the palace. They will be staying with us until the storms pass."

She nodded, looking at me sweetly. I could think of worse fates than being stuck in a palace for the rest of the winter with four gorgeous women all nearly my age. Maybe this trip wasn't so full of pain after all.

Leira hushed her voice. "Are you coming, Kadin? Or are you just going to stand there, gawking?"

Thankfully, she didn't say it loud enough for anyone else to hear. "I wasn't gawking," I muttered, following after Michi.

"Yeah, right," Leira scoffed.

Gaius grinned as I walked past him. "Yes you were."

How a blind man would know that was beyond me.

◆ ◆ ◆ ◆

As Michi led us past the Door of the Phoenix, I asked her if we could look inside.

"Oh, no." Her voice was as delicate as the song of a bird. "But when you're ready, perhaps, yes."

"When I'm ready?"

She looked at me intensely. "It can be quite a shock unless you're ready. Once you go in, all four doors inside the Hall of Tales must be opened and entered before you can leave. Some people have stayed trapped in there for years trying to get up enough courage to open the fourth door." She glanced from me to Leira. "The Door of the Phoenix thought they were ready, but I daresay they were not prepared to see what the castle had to show them."

Trapped for years?

I guess not.

Michi led us down one warmly lit corridor after another until we came to a room at the north end of the castle.

"Michi?" I said.

"Yes?"

"If Gaius is blind, how did he know you'd entered the commons? How did he know when or where to bow?"

"He heard my dress rustle."

"But he called you by name. How did he know it was you and not one of your sisters?"

"He can hear the difference between the colors," she replied matter-of-factly.

"Oh."

Okay. That's impressive.

Michi reached for the handle of the door in front of us. "This is where I work."

Above the door was a plaque that read:

Truth is not a tamed beast to bridle as you please.
Truth is wild and runs and pants
and leaps and climbs and breathes.

She opened the door, and the three of us stepped inside. Michi's study was small and simply decorated. Several paintings hung on the walls—scenes of snowcapped mountains and glistening rivers. They were signed in an elegant script with Gaius's name.

Michi's desk sat below a window overlooking the valley. Glass had been fastened in place to provide light for her work and protection from the wind. Even now, as snow pelted the window, we remained dry and warm. A mirror hung from the wall adjacent to the window. On Michi's desk were two Books of Blood flipped open, a large ink blotter, and several quill pens. One of the books had writing on one side only, the other on both. I walked over to look at them more carefully.

"My sisters and I are scribes," Michi explained, "in the service of the king."

Leira joined me. "So you copy the books and then give them to Alcion and his friends to share throughout the kingdom?"

Michi nodded. "Yes. So that others can hear the ancient tales and, if they wish, begin their journeys to Celestia."

I laid my hand against the book she was still copying and could feel its warmth and the gentle pulsing of its living pages. "Is it true the words are written in blood?" I managed to ask at last, glancing at the ink well inset in her desk, hoping it wasn't filled with what I suspected.

"It is."

Leira and I were quiet.

The next question was obvious, but it was not one that either Leira or I wanted to ask: *But whose blood fills those pages?*

"Well," Michi said, "Shall we go?"

She showed us the rooms where her sisters worked. Each study was similarly equipped with a desk containing writing quills and two books—one with the words they had copied and the other with the original. Each room also had a mirror, and paintings signed by Gaius.

"Did he paint those before he became blind?" I asked.

"He was born blind," Michi responded.

"But then how does he paint?"

"We describe the mountains to him and he paints what he sees in his mind. I told you, he can hear the difference between the colors."

"But what about the portraits of people in the hall?" Leira asked. "Did he paint those as well?"

"Yes." Michi lowered her eyes. "The paintings in the hallway are the portraits of those who have died in the service of the king. Gaius paints them from our descriptions so those vagabonds will not be forgotten."

A moment passed, and it seemed to be a small way of grieving the dead. Footsteps broke the silence and we turned to see Shika arrive.

She asked Michi something in Serecean, and Michi responded in kind. Then Leira said something to them both, and they were obviously pleased that she knew the language. While they talked, I stood by, waiting somewhat awkwardly for them to be done. Finally I asked Leira what they were talking about.

"I asked them if they ever leave the castle."

Shika nodded. "And we told her that we have each made a vow to stay here and work for the king until the day he calls for us to visit Celestia."

"I'll bet you get lonely up here sometimes?" I ventured, looking first at Shika, then at Michi.

"Sometimes," Michi admitted with a smile. "So we always enjoy company."

"I could think of a lot of guys who might make a journey all the way here just to meet the three of you." I meant it only as an innocent compliment.

Leira just shook her head: *Oh please.*

Shika and Michi exchanged light smiles.

Leira cleared her throat. "So, isn't it about time for supper?"

"I believe it is," Shika said with a bow. I bowed back to her enthusiastically and followed her and her sister to the dining area.

Leira grunted and brought up the rear.

CHAPTER TWELVE

Visions

I don't know how long we stayed at that beautiful castle waiting for the fury of winter to pass. Sometimes, when I think about those days, it seems like I spent a whole lifetime in that mysterious place. Other times it seems like the season passed in a single day.

Though I wasn't sure of the length of our stay, I do know that the longer we were there, the more time itself began to seem like a foreign concept, like a childish notion that we were finally growing out of. The moments ran together like ripples of water overtaking each other on a lake. Was it a month or a year or a handful of days that we were there at that glass-and-stone palace? Looking back now, I can hardly say.

Shika and Leira became close friends during our stay and spoke together often in Serecean. Leira and I also became closer. We learned many sayings from Gaius and many stories from the sisters. Asvina was an amazing storyteller and had committed most of the Book of Blood to memory. Often in the evenings, as we sat by the fireplace, she would recite stories from the book, with occasional commentary by Gaius.

In those days, Alcion taught us a song he said he'd learned long ago in the courts of King Kiral himself. He often hummed the tune to himself as he walked the halls of the outpost. And though he taught us the melody, he never taught us the words. "You'll learn them someday," he would tell us, "but I'm not the one to teach you."

One morning, when I noticed the first signs of spring appearing outside, I went looking for Leira to see if she'd like to take a walk. When I couldn't find her, I decided to check if the three sisters might know where she was.

I knocked on Shika's door and found it unlocked. When I pressed it open, I saw her standing in front of her mirror with her back turned to me. "Shika, have you seen Leira?" I asked. "I wanted to see if she'd like to go for a—"

But the person who whirled around to face me was not Shika.

"Leira? What are you doing in here? Why are you wearing Shika's dress?"

"Oh, please, Kadin." Her face was flushed. "Don't tell the sisters. You mustn't tell."

"But what's going on? What are you doing?"

"It's just that they look so beautiful, and I . . . I wanted to see how it would feel to look like that . . . Promise me you won't tell them. I would be too ashamed."

"Okay," I said. "No problem." It shocked me that Leira didn't think of herself as pretty, but then I remembered her difficult childhood and her ordeal in the baron's dungeon. I realized that it was only natural to doubt your beauty when you'd experienced that much pain. "But if you're up for a walk, get changed. I'll meet you on the trail by the main entrance."

After changing into her own clothes she joined me outside, and for the rest of the afternoon we explored the mountaintop trails, enjoying the warm weather and the fresh taste of springtime in the air. The day slipped by, and we were late returning to the castle.

We missed dinner and hurried toward the fireplace in the commons for Asvina's tales. As we passed the Door of the Phoenix we saw Alcion stepping into the hall and closing the door behind him.

"Alcion," I called, "join us by the fireplace."

Only then did I notice how pale and deeply troubled he looked.

"Alcion? Are you okay?"

My friend nodded slowly. "I don't think I can make it tonight, Kadin. I have an appointment to keep in Wyckell, a nearby city, that I . . . have to prepare for."

"What kind of appointment?"

He ignored my question, and when he spoke he seemed distracted. "All vagabonds must pass through Wyckell, one way or another. Join me there in two days, would you? Both of you?"

Leira and I readily agreed. "Of course," I said.

"I'll meet you at the home of Mnason."

"Sure. All right."

Alcion remained strangely quiet.

"Are you sure everything's okay?" I asked again.

"It will be soon," he answered cryptically. "Soon . . . so, Mnason's house, then." He smiled and seemed to regain his composure.

"Yes," I told him. "Mnason's house. Two days."

Before he left, Alcion glanced from me to Leira. "Listen carefully, my friends. The people in Wyckell will do all they can to make you feel at home. They'll invite you to their parties, to their stores, to their homes. And there will always be one more trinket to buy, one more party to attend, one more cup to drink."

"They enjoy themselves," I said.

"Oh yes."

"Is there something wrong with that?" Leira asked.

"There's nothing wrong with joy, but you mustn't become too comfortable in Wyckell. Remember, you're only passing through. Travel lightly. It's easy to get distracted there, and the more you entangle yourself with those people, the more their way of life will entangle you. Some vagabonds on their way to Celestia have paused there to rest and never made it any further."

"We'll be careful," I promised.

Leira nodded.

Alcion seemed so tired.

"Are you sure nothing's wrong?" I pressed him.

He placed his hand on my shoulder. "I'll see you in Wyckell, then."

And then Alcion walked slowly away, humming the hauntingly beautiful song he had learned in the courtyard of the king. The music echoed around us in the dim chamber and then slowly faded away.

When he was gone, Leira said, "Okay, that was odd."

"I don't like it. Something's not right."

Just then Michi appeared at the end of the corridor. "The fire has been lit," she said politely. "Are you still planning to join us? Asvina was wondering if she should begin the tales without you."

"We're coming," I called. "We'll be right there."

After Michi had bowed and walked away, I turned to Leira and pointed to the Door of the Phoenix. "Afterward, though, we go in there to see what disturbed Alcion."

"Do you think the door will open for us?"

"I don't know, but if the door doesn't open for us—"

"You mean if it doesn't think we're ready?"

"Right, we'll find another way in. Something's bothering Alcion and I want to know what it is before we leave for Wyckell."

We glanced at the door once more before leaving. Thin threads of mist curled from beneath it while, on the other side of it, something moaned.

Then we left to join the others at the fireplace.

◆ ◆ ◆ ◆

Leira and I grabbed some bread to munch on and sat between Shika and Michi at the fire. Gaius ambled up with a mug of ale and plopped down beside Shika. He mumbled something about good stories needing good refreshment, and then we were all quiet.

Firelight flickered off Asvina's face and glimmered off her green dress as she slid another log into the fire and began her tale.

"A thousand years ago, all of the land from the Scaldian

Mountains to the Rylekian Sea was under the rule of one king—a great and wise king. He was gracious to his subjects, and there was peace in the land. But one of his knights became envious of the king's power and wanted to rule the kingdom himself. He hatched a plot to kill the king and take over the land. One day he dipped the tip of his dagger into poison made from the venom of Baskian vipers and waited in hiding for the king. Fortunately, the king's bodyguards caught the knight in the throne room with the poisoned dagger before he could carry out his plan. The royal counselors advised the king to execute the would-be assassin, but the king was merciful. In honor of the knight's previous years of service, he didn't have him killed but rather banished forever from Celestia."

I tried to remember the names of some of these characters. I'd read about them in the Book of Blood, but now the names and dates and details eluded me.

Asvina continued. "Soon the mutinous knight began circulating lies about the king. They spread like a disease throughout the kingdom. More and more of the king's subjects joined the knight's cause—secretly at first, then openly, as they were lured by the knight's promises of wealth and comfort and power, if only he were on the throne. The knight eventually formed an alliance with a dark wizard named Killius, who some say commanded an entire army of ghouls from the underworld. Even the king's vizier joined them."

"What's a vizier?" I whispered to Leira.

"A chancellor," she explained, "or a head of state."

I nodded.

The fire crackled and leapt before us. Transfixed, we all stared into the flames as we listened to Asvina's mesmerizing voice. "Secretly, the vizier brought the knight the very keys to the king's castle in Celestia. He and the king were the only two who could issue royal decrees, for they alone wore signet rings of Celestia."

She paused and I remembered my pardon with the wax seal bearing the current king of Celestia's imprint.

"The vizier slipped away, and the king learned of the treachery. He sent envoys to reason with the rebels, but his messengers were tortured, imprisoned, or killed by the rebel knight and Killius—you've seen portraits of some of those ambassadors lining the halls of this palace. At last the king decided to send his knights—all of them—to raid the insurgents' outpost and slaughter all of the wicked traitors. But that's when the king's son, the prince, offered to go himself to reason with them."

"But why?" I said. "I don't understand. They were traitors. They deserved to die for their crimes."

"Yes," Asvina replied. "That's what the king said. But many people had joined the wicked knight, and in the end, his son convinced him that it was worth one last try before destroying them all. 'Mercy before bloodshed,' said the prince. That was his motto—"

"Mercy before bloodshed," Shika and Michi said reverently.

"Mercy before bloodshed," Gaius repeated.

"At last," Asvina went on, "the prince went to negotiate the rebels' surrender. Though he was a mighty warrior he appeared before them with no weapons—"

"No weapons," Gaius said.

"No weapons," echoed the sisters.

"No weapons," I said, trying to make it seem like I knew what I was doing.

The sisters and Gaius turned to me with incredulous looks on their faces.

"We only say it two extra times," Michi whispered. "Not three."

"Oh."

"Please continue, Asvina," grumbled Gaius.

"So the prince appeared before them, and while speaking to the renegade knight, he was attacked from behind by the wizard Killius and his apprentices. The prince was wounded, but was able to kill the dark wizard and twelve of his lords with the sword from his own belt—"

"I thought he was unarmed?" I said.

"From the *wizard's* belt," she corrected. "Remember, the prince had appeared before them with no weapons—"

"No weapons," I exclaimed. But no one replied. They all stared at me.

"We only do it once for each saying," Michi said.

"Oh. I see."

Asvina smiled. "So, the prince stopped the rebellion, retrieved the keys to Celestia, and was even able to kill the wizard—"

"Some say Killius survived," Gaius interrupted.

Asvina hesitated. "Yes, but I believe from my readings of the book that he did not."

"What happened to the rebel knight and the king's vizier?" Leira asked.

"It's a little unclear, but it appears that the vizier killed the knight and escaped. Then the vizier disappeared, but we believe he fled to a distant land, took on a new name, and moved west."

"Of course, in the process of fighting Killius, much of the prince's own blood was shed. Some say he died and was brought back to life solely by the depth of his father's love—"

"His father's love," I said.

"His father's love," said Leira.

Our four friends stared at us. "We don't do that line," Gaius explained.

"Oh. Sorry."

But then Gaius smiled. "Although maybe we could add it. It's a good one."

Asvina concluded her story, "And now, the prince has returned to the city of Celestia where he lives with his father, King Kiral."

The sisters nodded.

The fire danced.

And I stared at Asvina unbelievingly. "What?" I said at last. "King Kiral? But he's the king *now.* I thought that story happened a thousand years ago? Does the same king still live today?"

"Of course," Asvina said.

"You'll meet him for yourself when you arrive at the city," Michi added.

It didn't make sense. "But how? How could he live for a thousand years?"

Shika leaned forward. "Stop thinking of time as a series of events that happen one after another. There are places where time doesn't happen in order, but all at once."

Michi must have seen the confusion on my face because she said, "If you were on a high mountain watching a line of soldiers returning from war you would see them all at once, the entire legion stretching through the valley. But if you were sitting beside the road you would only see them pass by one at a time—you wouldn't be able to see those at the beginning, nor those at the end. However, from the mountaintop you would see all: the beginning, the middle, and the end of the line at the same time."

Asvina agreed. "Time has less to do with the progression of events than the perspective from which you watch them occur."

Part of me could understand what the sisters were saying, but part of me was still puzzled. How could time not happen in order? These three sisters seemed amazingly wise for their age. "So in that land—in this land—everything happens at the same time?"

"Of course not," Gaius said a bit gruffly. "It isn't for your mind to understand but for your heart to believe." Then he stared with his sightless eyes into my seeing ones. "Faith doesn't mean knowing the answers but trusting your way through the questions."

Before I could ask him to clarify a bit more, he rose from

his chair and announced it was time for all of us to get some sleep. Then he lumbered off toward his room.

As the sisters were getting up to leave, I had an unsettling thought. I asked Shika to stay for a moment. "How long have you and your sisters been working at this castle?"

"As we said, time is different here on this mountain. You have to understand that."

"Yes. I know, but I'm just wondering. How old are you?"

"It's different here, Kadin," she said again, somewhat uneasily.

Leira grinned a little then, though I couldn't guess why. She said something in Serecean to Shika, who nodded and replied in the same foreign tongue.

I pressed Shika for an answer and finally she sighed and said, "I'm closing in on nine hundred years here next March."

I blinked.

Nine *hundred?*

I blinked again.

Then, Shika bowed to me and backed out of the room.

Leira laughed and poked me good-naturedly on the arm. "I'd say she's a little old for you, hero. Better stick to girls from your own century."

Asvina and Michi were giggling in the hallway.

"I'll meet you in a half hour by the Door of the Phoenix," I muttered to Leira who just wouldn't stop smiling. Then I added, "That's a half-hour *normal* time."

When I left, I could still hear the girls trying to stifle their laughter.

◆ ◆ ◆ ◆

Half an hour later, Leira was at the door to the Hall of Tales waiting for me when I arrived. Apparently the others had gone to bed.

"Ready?" I asked.

She nodded, still smiling.

"They hide their age well," I said defensively. "How long have you known?"

"Most of the winter."

"Why didn't you say something?"

"It was more fun watching you flirt with elderly women."

"Great." I put my hand on the door handle. "Well anyway, here goes." The moment I tried the door, the latch clicked, and the Door of the Phoenix swung open.

"Well," Leira said, "I guess we're ready."

"At least the castle thinks so."

Both Leira and I peered inside. The Hall of Tales was eerily lit by pale moonlight that filtered through the glass-filled cracks. Mist curled from beneath the four doors, two of which lay on each side of the hall.

I hesitated before entering, remembering that some people had spent years trying to get up enough nerve to open all the doors of the hallway that stretched before us.

Leira stepped back. "I'm not so sure about this place."

"You want to find out what upset Alcion, don't you?"

"Well . . . yes."

"Come on, then. It can't be that bad."

"That's what you said about the voices in Apollyon's cave."

"And see how well that turned out?"

"Right."

At last, gathering my courage, I entered the Hall of Tales.

Leira followed me and the door behind us closed by itself. For a moment I wondered if maybe the castle itself believed in magik even if its occupants did not.

One hallway.

Two doors on each side.

I walked up to the first door on the right. "Stay here. I'll go first."

"Well, if you insist."

I opened the door.

Stepped inside.

This door, just like the first, closed by itself behind me. Immediately, I suspected that this was the room from which I'd heard the moans earlier. Instead of seeing a castle room as I expected, I stood in a graveyard cluttered with crooked and ancient tombstones and freshly dug, open graves. Fog curled through the damp night. Wandering among the tombs and graves were people of all ages moaning as if they were the living dead. Curls of darkness slithered from the open graves like wisps of smoke, popping and sizzling as they groped at the dim moonlight and then retreated into the tombs, only to reach out again.

Just like the darkness had done in the cave beyond Apollyon's lair.

A few of the walking dead turned toward me, sniffing at the air, then letting out unearthly shrieks. In the moonlight, I saw their faces, and a chill ran down my spine.

All of them were missing their eyes.

Get out of here, Kadin.

Beyond them I noticed a gate on the other side of the graveyard. Though it looked metal, somehow I could see through it and the elegantly curved letters read:

⅃⅃ƎꓘƆYW

Wyckell.

The city where Alcion had told us to meet him.

As I was trying to process this, all of the living dead faced me and began staggering in my direction. I stumbled back to the door and reached for the handle. Thankfully, the door swung open, and I burst into the hallway, slammed it shut behind me, and leaned hard against it.

"What happened?" Leira stared at me. "You look like you saw a ghost."

"That's not a good door. We'll leave that one closed."

"Do you think that's the room that disturbed Alcion?"

I took a deep breath. "Could be."

"But what did you see? You were only gone a second or two."

Her words surprised me. I knew I'd been in there much longer than a few seconds. I was about to say something when she took a step forward. "Let me look."

I waved her back. "I don't think that's such a good idea. I think we should get out of here."

"We can't. We haven't tried the other doors."

Just in case, I went to the Door of the Phoenix and yanked, but it didn't budge.

"Remember what Michi said? We can't leave until all four doors have been opened."

"Right," I said, my heart sinking, "and entered."

"You don't look so good. Let me try the next one."

"No. I'll—"

"I'll be all right," she assured me. And before I could stop her, she'd paced across the hallway and opened the door across from the one I'd entered. It slammed shut behind her and a moment later, reopened again. Leira closed the door, wide-eyed and panting.

"Did you see anything?"

She nodded.

"But you weren't gone long enough to," I objected.

"I was in there at least fifteen minutes!"

I shook my head. "That's impossible, Leira. You weren't in there more than a few—"

"Forget how long I was in the room!"

"Sorry. Um . . . what did you see?"

She was still breathing heavily. "A woman with a rake. I could only see her from behind. She was scratching the rake across the floor, though there wasn't much to rake up, just straw and a few small sticks. Then a man appeared between us and offered her a crown. I couldn't see his face, but he was dressed nobly, like a prince or a king. He looked like he was calling to the woman, but she didn't hear him or turn around. She leaned down toward the dirt and when she looked up, she turned toward me and I saw her face . . ."

Remembering the walking dead who had no eyes, I said nervously, "What was it like?"

"It was me, Kadin. I was the one with the rake. What do you think it means?"

"I don't know." I was thankful that at least her room hadn't been as disturbing at the one I'd entered. However, it had still obviously upset her

Both of us stared down the hallway. "Two more doors," she said.

"Maybe we weren't ready to come in here after all."

"The castle thought we were."

"According to Michi it's been wrong before."

Once again I remembered Michi's words, *"Some people have stayed trapped in there for years trying to get up enough courage to open the last door."*

"All right," I said. "Here goes." I approached the door next to the one Leira had just opened, took a deep breath, pressed my hand against it. With a slight creak the door eased open, and I stepped into the third room.

The door closed.

This room was nothing like the first. In fact, it actually looked like a normal room you might find in a castle. Thankfully, it didn't contain any walking corpses or open graves.

The furniture, the floor, the shelves, the window sills—everything was blanketed with a thick layer of dust. While I watched, a woman appeared as if from nowhere and began to sweep. The more she swept the room, the more the dust swirled into the air and choked her. The more she choked on the dust, the more desperately she swept the room, which only made her condition worse.

Suddenly, water came rushing from above where the walls met the ceiling, as if the room was underwater and someone had suddenly lifted the ceiling just enough to let the water in. It poured down the walls and across the floor and through the room, cleansing everything. Then it disappeared. The water washed the woman as well. Though drenched, she let out a sigh of relief, found a door on the other side of the room, opened it, and strode into the warm light of a spring day. As she closed the door behind her, the furniture began to disappear until at last the room was empty.

Curious.

I returned to the Hall of Tales. "That one wasn't so bad."

Leira was shaking.

"What's wrong?"

"I opened the last door," she whispered.

"What!"

"While you went in there. I thought it would save time." She swallowed hard and looked at me intensely. "Kadin, Alcion is in danger. We have to stop him from going to Wyckell."

"How do you know? What did you see in that room?"

She told me, and I agreed. We had to stop Alcion right away, before it was too late.

The room contained a foreshadowing of his death.

We turned and bolted out of the Hall of Tales.

◆ ◆ ◆ ◆

As we burst through the Door of the Phoenix I was surprised to see sunlight filling the rest of the castle.

"We couldn't have been in there all night," I muttered. "What's going on?"

We hurried to Alcion's room, but when we arrived we found it empty, save for a note: *See you in Wyckell. Be careful.*

"We're too late," Leira gasped. "He left without us."

"Then we have to find him there, at Mnason's home. And we'd better hurry."

We quickly packed for our trip. Shika caught up with us in the main hallway as we were about to leave. "There you are," she said. "You've been to the Hall of Tales, haven't you?"

"How did you know?" Leira asked.

"You disappeared four days ago—"

I stared at her. "What?"

"We told you time is different here."

"But Alcion is in danger," Leira said. "He told us to meet him in two days and we've been in—"

"Where did he go?"

"Wyckell."

"Oh, no," Shika whispered.

Gaius appeared at the end of the corridor. "I heard him leave on horseback the morning after you two disappeared. I didn't know he had left for the fair—"

The fair must be in Wyckell.

"You can take horses too," Shika said quickly. While her sisters left to saddle the steeds, she asked us, "You do know how to ride, don't you?"

Leira nodded.

I bit my lip.

Shika noticed. "Can you ride, Kadin? If you walk, you may not reach him until it's too late."

"Sure," I said. "I can ride."

Leira stared at me. "Have you ever ridden a horse before?"

"Well, not exactly," I admitted.

"It's easy," Gaius assured me. "You'll learn in no time." It might have surprised me that a blind man knew how to ride a horse, but since it was Gaius it didn't surprise me at all. "These are not typically horses."

Shika led us outside, where Asvina was finishing saddling the second mount. Leira and I strapped our packs and my walking stick to the sides of the saddles, and after some riding instructions from Gaius and Shika, and directions to Wyckell from Asvina, we mounted the steeds.

As we were saying goodbye, Michi came running up carrying our pardons, which I'd accidentally left in my room.

"Don't forget these," she said urgently. "You'll need them to gain entrance into Celestia."

"Those who come without his invitation will leave without his mercy," Gaius offered. And then as we were leaving, he called out one final warning, "The river is not as deep as the valley!"

"What did that mean?" I asked Leira.

"I have no idea," she said, but we nodded and waved like we understood and then spurred on our horses.

I clung apprehensively to the reins, but the horse seemed to know I was inexperienced and the ride was surprisingly smooth.

Winter may have been passing into spring, but dark clouds hung heavy and low on the horizon as we sped toward Wyckell.

CHAPTER THIRTEEN

Despite my initial discomfort, we made good time riding the horses. I didn't fall off once, and as the day wore on, I became more and more at ease in the saddle. Perhaps my horse was enchanted. I began to encourage her. "Good girl," I told her. "Thanks for taking it easy on me."

Leira heard me. "Who are you talking to?"

"I thought maybe the horse could understand me. After all, this is a land where walking sticks start fires, rooms tell tales, and books turn into axes that cut through stone. Maybe animals can understand human words."

At that, the horse whinnied, and I patted her. "See, I knew you could understand me, girl."

Leira just shook her head and rode on ahead of us. "I think you've been on the trail too long."

"Don't mind her," I told my horse as we trotted up the trail. "She gets moody sometimes."

As Leira and I rode into and out of the spring showers, I thought back to what she'd told me about the last room in the Hall of Tales, the one concerning Alcion's death. "There were two men standing before a large crowd," Leira had said. "I couldn't see their faces, but I could tell the crowd was angry. They started yelling, then they became enraged and began to pick up rocks and throw them at the two men. I cried out for them to stop, but they wouldn't. When they were finally finished, I rushed up to the two men. I tossed the rocks aside and saw the face of the first—"

My heart was beating fast. "Who was it?"

"Alcion. And he wasn't moving. He was dead, Kadin. So I turned to the other man. He seemed to be breathing, but it was hard to tell. My hand was shaking as I rolled him over. Then I saw his face. It was . . ."

I said nothing, but I was thinking about her vision of the woman with the rake, the woman that'd turned out to be her. I hoped I was not the other man lying on the ground.

It was a long time before she went on. "It was the prince from my dream," she said at last.

I felt a wash of thankfulness that it wasn't me, but then I was overcome with the thought that this prince from her dreams might be a real person, just as Alcion is. "What dream, Leira?"

"It doesn't matter. The point is, Alcion is in danger."

Though curious, I hadn't pressed her about the dream.

Now as I thought about that room, I wondered if we would be able to reach Alcion in time. "Faster, girl," I said to my horse.

She snorted and galloped down the road.

◆ ◆ ◆ ◆

As Leira and I approached the outskirts of Wyckell, I could see right away that it was much larger than Abaddon, and yet, surprisingly, there were no protective walls around it. It hadn't been designed to keep marauders out, but rather to draw in anyone who might be passing by.

And, while we hadn't met many other travelers on our trip so far, we began to see more and more people now. Some infected, some healed. Some on horseback, many on foot. Everyone seemed friendly and welcoming and excited to be traveling to Wyckell. Dozens of roads converged here, leading into the main thoroughfare to the city. Based on the different skin colors and apparel, it was clear that people were traveling to this city from all across the kingdom.

On the outskirts of Wyckell we found merchants with carts of apples and hay for tired horses and piles of clothes and fresh food for weary travelers.

After allowing our horses a small snack, we entered the city.

The roads and buildings of Wyckell had been designed by someone with an eye for beauty as well as commerce. Most of the structures were made of stone gathered from the high plains and boulder-strewn fields surrounding the city. Many buildings were elaborate and ornate, but even the most modest homes were more beautiful than any I'd seen in Abaddon. The wide, spacious streets could be navigated easily by two or even three carriages at once. On the horizon, faraway mountains created a panoramic backdrop for the resplendent town.

Temples built in honor of a legion of gods and goddesses adorned the main streets of Wyckell. Numerous priests and priestesses in their distinctive gowns, capes, and tunics moved noiselessly between the buildings. Apparently they were here to help the townspeople worship whatever god they chose in whatever way they wished. A series of brothels and taverns were conveniently located beside the temples to make it even easier to indulge in any type of worship you desired. I noticed one temple had a life-sized statue of Apollyon on its steps. Great cries and shouts came spewing from the entrance of the temple as we slowly rode past.

"Something big is going on in there," Leira observed. "I wonder if they know what happened to their god?"

"I hope not."

As we passed, I noticed a tall figure wearing a hooded tunic standing in the shadow of Apollyon's temple. But rather than gesticulating with the other worshippers, he was slowly scanning the streets. His eyes seemed to lock onto me, but since the hood shrouded his face in shadows, I couldn't be sure. There was something eerily familiar about the way he stood.

"We need to find Alcion," I said, "right away."

Leira nodded quietly, gazing at the displays of jewelry, scarves, and clothes lining the streets. My horse whinnied and stamped at the ground.

A dual network of interconnected canals crisscrossed the city, one which provided clean water for cooking and washing, the other which served as a discreet system for disposing of waste and refuse. Apparently the canal system also served to irrigate the lush fields that skirted the city. I'd never seen or heard of a town with such engineering and architectural marvels. Nothing like this could be found in the plains surrounding Abaddon. Nothing like this could be found anywhere.

We asked for directions to Mnason's house and were pointed eastward, where we now directed our horses.

He'll know where Alcion is. Find Mnason, and you'll find Alcion.

It didn't take us long to discover that the east side of the city contained the most impressive thing of all about Wyckell.

The fair.

As we approached, the first thing I noticed was the music. From nearly every tent, awning, pub, or home came the sound of drums or flutes or tambourines. And even though everyone seemed to be playing a different melody, all the notes somehow found their place in the same riotous, rollicking song. Rather than create dissonance, all the notes complemented each other, creating an alluring and inviting melody that made even me want to join in and dance.

This entire section of the city was a swirl of music and dancers and laughter and exotic fragrances rising in the afternoon sun. It all seemed so wonderful, so perfect.

"It's magnificent," Leira said.

I remembered Alcion's warning that some vagabonds on their way to Celestia have paused here to rest and never made it any further.

And now that I was here, I could see why.

She gazed around the streets. "So, where exactly did they say his house is?"

"Just that it's on this side of the city. We'll have to ask someone else for specifics."

I looked around for any vagabonds, anyone wearing the same kind of tunics or clothes that Leira and I had been given at the Inn. But in all the crowd of people, I saw very few wearing the distinctive garb of a vagabond.

As we rode along, people called out, offering us their goods, their services, their merchandise. Politely, I refused each of them. "Just passing through," I said, or "Sorry, not today." Some people nodded and smiled. Others did not look at all pleased that we weren't interested in taking part in their fair.

Suddenly, a short stout man with an enormous, curling mustache rode up beside us on a steed as black as night. "Guests of Wyckell!" he called, "I welcome you! You're not from around here, are you?"

I suspected he was just trying to lure me to his tent or store. "No." I avoided eye contact. "We're not."

He rode closer and whispered in a voice meant only for my ears, "On to Celestia, then?"

At that, I studied him more carefully. He was dressed in the typical colorful raiment of the city, not the clothes of a vagabond. "What do you know about Celestia?"

"All anyone can be expected to know, this side of the river." Then, loud enough for anyone passing by to hear, he announced, "I'm Jibben! Your humble guide to Wyckell, here to serve you!" He bowed, as much as one can bow while riding a horse.

"Did Alcion send you?" Leira asked suspiciously.

Jibben nodded enthusiastically. "Yes, yes, of course, Alcion! He told me all about you. I would have recognized you two anywhere by his description!"

"Alcion sent you to meet us?" I said in disbelief.

Jibben directed his horse closer to mine once again. "I'm here to escort you through the city. I expected you sooner."

To test him, I said, "So he told you whose house to take us to?"

Jibben looked from me to Leira. He hesitated for a moment and then shook his head. "Unfortunately, no, he did not. He told me you'd know where to go. That I should show you this and you would trust me." Jibben pulled the collar of his cloak to the side, revealing a small curved scar at the base of his neck.

"You're a vagabond?" Leira asked. "Yet you live here?"

"I'm a guide to vagabonds. I lead them through the city and help them to refresh their souls during their stay here in Wyckell."

"Is Alcion all right?" I asked.

"I saw him earlier today, and he was fine, but worried that you two had not yet arrived."

"Just a moment." I slowed my horse so that I was riding next to Leira, then asked her quietly, "Do you trust him?"

She shook her head. "No. But, it does make sense that Alcion would send someone here to greet us, to guide us. After all, he told us to meet him at Mnason's house—nothing more specific than that, not even where it is." She nodded toward Jibben. "At least he seems willing to help us." She was watching the women dance past us as she spoke.

"Okay, then. We go with him. But we watch our step."

Jibben was smiling and waving to the people of the city, who all seemed to recognize him.

I nudged my horse closer to his. "Mnason's house," I said to him. "Lead us there. That's where we meet Alcion."

Jibben smiled at me. "Yes, yes, Mnason's house. I should have known. Come, then. It's not far." He turned down a side street, and we spurred our horses on to follow him into the fair.

◆ ◆ ◆ ◆

As we entered the heart of Wyckell's fair, people dressed in every conceivable color and costume danced and twirled around us, sliding against each other in an uncontrollable frenzy of celebration to the beat of the pulsing, pumping music.

The music and activity made it difficult to speak, but every couple of minutes we came to a park or grove of trees that provided a brief respite from the noise.

Jibben told us that according to some people, Wyckell was founded over a thousand years ago, but that others said it was older than Celestia itself. "Every night there's a ball," he explained as we passed one of the wooded areas. "Or if you prefer more private entertainment, there are escorts available to grant your every wish, provide for your every desire, fulfill your every fantasy."

I nodded. I could see he was warning us, just as Alcion had warned us about becoming entangled in the life of Wyckell. My suspicions about Jibben began to subside somewhat, and I found myself believing that it really was likely Alcion had arranged for someone to meet us—and in the case of Jibben, someone familiar enough with the allurements and enticements of the city to be our guide.

The fair was a sweeping vista of jugglers and fire breathers, animal tamers and acrobats, artisans and stage actors, magicians and potters, sellers and buyers of anything your heart could ever desire. In nearby fields there were games of chance, luck, and skill. Carts full of spices and fruit and meat lined the streets and, as Jibben put it, everything was delicious and divine and always on sale. Ale flowed as freely as the water in the canals, and no one had a care in the world.

In contrast to the frivolity of the fair, I noticed a growing number of harsh-looking soldiers equipped with swords and crossbows, until finally they appeared at nearly every street corner.

Jibben smiled at them cordially as he told us under his breath, "Security is a little tighter than usual. They arrested someone this morning. They're keeping it all very quiet, but they claim he was a traitor who tried to assassinate the magistrate. The trial is tomorrow. Word is, they're looking for his conspirators."

As he said this, we passed a stout pole driven into the ground with wood piled around its base. I shivered as I remembered a similar post in Abaddon, set up to burn wizards and witches.

Overall, the swirling, frolicking colors and the flurry of thousands of people laughing and drinking and eating and dancing was enough to take your breath away.

"I've never seen anything else like this before," Leira said.

"There isn't anything like this," I said. Then, I turned to Jibben. "Does anyone here actually work for a living?"

He laughed. "This *is* their living, my friend. Call it work, call it play, call it what you will. To the people of Wyckell, it is called *life!* And if you ask them, there's no finer life anywhere in the world."

After so many nights of sleeping on rocks and forest floors, of being wary of danger at every bend, of eating meager scraps of meat and bread, I could think of nothing more appealing than spending a few days here in Wyckell recuperating, relaxing, and enjoying myself again.

But then I remembered Alcion and the visions Leira and I had seen in the Hall of Tales. *Stay focused, Kadin,* I told myself. *Don't get distracted.*

"We're here," Jibben said at last, pulling his horse to a stop in front of an inn.

"This is where he lives?" I asked.

"No. But I need to speak to someone, make sure it's safe for you to visit his home." He dismounted and hustled inside.

Leira turned to me. "So what do you think?"

"I don't know. I'm not sure I trust him, but I don't know who to trust. He *is* a vagabond."

"Or *was* one," Leira said.

Her words didn't exactly reassure me.

While we waited, some of the merchants of Wyckell offered us trinkets and clothing, which I respectfully declined. I thanked them for their offers but told them I wasn't shopping for anything today.

A pale man with sunken eyes approached my horse and reached into his coat. "You're dressed like a vagabond," he murmured.

"Yes."

He pulled a pardon out of his pocket. "You'll need one of these to get into Celestia." The words oozed from his mouth like blood from an infected sore. "I have the best prices in town."

"No thank you."

He didn't like my answer, but I finally convinced him I was not in the market to buy one of his pardons. However, I kept from offering the information that I already had one. For a reason I couldn't quite pinpoint, it didn't seem like that would have been a good thing to say.

At last he scowled and slinked away. I turned to warn Leira that we'd better get moving, but when I did, I saw she'd dismounted and was admiring some jewelry at a roadside stand. The seller was nodding enthusiastically and beaming at her. To my surprise, Leira reached into her tunic and produced a coin. She handed it to the man, and he passed a silver bracelet to her.

Then she returned to her horse.

"What are you doing?" I asked under my breath.

"We don't want to attract attention." She turned her wrist to observe the bracelet from different angles. "I'm just trying to fit in."

I was telling her that I wasn't sure that was a good idea when Jibben emerged from the doorway and hurried over to us.

He shook his head and whispered, "My friend tells me Mnason's house is being watched. Something's wrong. You can stay here instead. It's a popular inn. No one will suspect anything. I'll be back to meet up with you first thing in the morning."

"No. We're supposed to meet Alcion—"

"In the morning. I promise you." He turned to leave.

"Where are you going?" I asked.

"I have to take care of a few things," he said evasively, but then smiled broadly and patted the flank of my horse. "I'll see you in the morning."

More people were beginning to look my way and I realized

Leira was right—at least for the moment fitting in seemed like a good idea. "Okay," I told Jibben. "First thing in the morning."

He nodded, glanced momentarily at Leira's glittering new purchase, hopped onto his horse and rode away, calling out boisterous greetings to all those he knew in the streets.

Leira and I left our horses tethered to the post outside the building, then walked inside, passed through a dimly lit tavern, and came to an unkempt man standing behind a check-in counter for the rooms to the inn. He was bald and sweaty and had big teeth and narrow eyes.

"We need two rooms for tonight," I said.

"Two rooms." The man looked back and forth from me to Leira. "And you do have some way to pay for your rooms?"

"Of course." I reached into my pack and produced a handful of the coins I'd carried all the way from Abaddon.

When I showed him my money he took one of the coins and skillfully flipped it through his fingers, weaving it over and over, end over end. Then he held it up to the light and studied it carefully. "Haven't seen this style of coin in a long time," he chuckled. "Where did you get it? Steal it from some poor vagabond?"

"I brought it with me," I replied. "It's from my hometown."

He eyed me suspiciously. "You're from the western plains?"

"Yes. Abaddon. Both of us are from there." I nodded toward Leira, but immediately wondered if sharing all of this was really such a good idea. Leira smiled at him politely. He gazed at her slowly, letting his eyes crawl down her body.

When I saw his leering looks, I dropped two more coins onto the counter to refocus his attention. "So will this be enough then?"

He eyed the coins, scooped them into his hand and wrapped his fingers tightly around them. "It'll be enough," he said, "for tonight." He handed me a key and then stretched out his hand, tilted his head cordially, and handed the other key to Leira. "Second floor. Enjoy your stay."

We took our keys and headed up the winding, narrow staircase to our rooms.

"I don't like him," I said. "I don't like this place, this inn, this town. We need to find Alcion and get out of here."

"Relax. It's going to be okay. Jibben will meet us tomorrow, and we'll find Mnason's house and meet up with Alcion. Until then, there's nothing we can do about it. Right?"

"We could look for him."

"Jibben said Mnason's house was being watched. Do you really think it's a good idea? We might attract the wrong kind of attention to both him and Alcion." She paused. "Right?"

I gave in. "I suppose you're right."

"So let's get unpacked and relax a little."

"Okay. We rest tonight, rise early. Wait for Jibben and then—"

"Actually, I think I'll go for a little walk. Stretch my legs."

"Leira, I think we should stay here."

"I'll be okay."

"Leira—"

"I'll be okay," she said stiffly. "I'm a big girl. I can take care of myself."

"I know, but . . ."

Her jaw was set, and I realized I'd better not push the issue. "Okay, I'm sorry. Um, just be careful."

"I've been sitting on a horse for hours. I just need some exercise. I'll see you at supper."

She left; I deposited my things in my room and then tried to take a nap, but I couldn't sleep. Wondering if the Book of Blood might mention Mnason's house, I spent the rest of the afternoon reading through it. His name never appeared.

That night, I ate alone. Leira didn't show up.

Finally, about an hour after I'd finished eating, she returned, adorned with earrings, bracelets, and a glittering necklace. I was waiting for her downstairs in the tavern, and when she walked in, a few of the men looked up from their drinks and gazed at her.

"You've been to the fair," I said.

She laughed. "Aren't they beautiful? I've never had anything like these before, Kadin. Never!" She twirled in front of me drawing grins from the drunken men at the nearby tables. "Oh, Kadin, I feel like a princess!"

I remembered how she had tried on Shika's dress, how she'd doubted her beauty, believed she was worthless, and I was torn between admiring her purchases and reminding her about Alcion's warnings about this town. Feeling awkward telling her how pretty she was—not just now but all the time—I said simply, "They are beautiful, yes." I lowered my voice. "Remember, we're just passing through here."

"Can we stay just for a while?" She was speaking loud enough to draw undue attention to us. "Just for a week or two before moving on?"

I rose. "We need to find Alcion—"

"Oh, we have to stay, Kadin!"

"Leira, listen to yourself. You're—"

A few large men at a nearby table shifted in their seats and glared at me. I whispered, "Alcion warned us about this place. Remember? He said to be careful. And remember what you saw in the Hall of Tales? The reason we came here?"

Leira's eyes turned icy. "Don't talk that way to me. Yes. I remember. I was just having a little fun."

By then I'd lost my patience. I didn't like the looks I was getting from the other men in the room, so I took her arm and hurried her upstairs. "We have to stay focused here. We need to find Alcion as quickly as possible and get out of this city."

She pulled back from me at the top of the stairs. "Maybe I don't want to leave. Maybe you and Alcion can go. Maybe I want to stay here for a while."

"What? Listen to what you're saying."

She turned and paced toward her room, scratching at the scar on her neck. Abruptly, she tossed open the door, entered, and slammed it behind her. Then I heard it lock.

I stood there in shock.

Over the next hour I knocked on her door more than a dozen times, but she wouldn't open it to me, wouldn't even answer when I called to her.

Finally I crawled into bed. *Maybe she just needs some sleep. You can sort it all out in the morning,* but part of me didn't really believe that at all.

It didn't take long for me to notice that the fair in Wyckell didn't slow down at night. If anything, it became even louder, even wilder. But it didn't really matter—I couldn't sleep anyway. I just lay there thinking about Leira.

About an hour before daybreak I was dozing when I heard coarse laughter outside my door. Then the click of a key in a lock. When the handle to my room didn't turn, I realized someone must be at the door across the hall.

Leira's room.

I jumped out of bed and rushed to the door, opened it a crack, and peered into the hall. Half a dozen men stood huddled around Leira's door. I wanted to drive them away, but I knew I could never fight that many. "Jibben," I muttered under my breath, "I never should have trusted you."

Do something, Kadin.

Distract them—

Before I could make a move, they eased Leira's door open. I couldn't see all their faces, but I heard the man who had checked us in earlier. He sounded scared. "I tell you she rented this room. I wouldn't lie to you."

There was a burst of curses; then another voice: "Well, it's empty now, you fool. Give me back my money. If you ever waste my time again, I'll feed you the tip of a dagger. Understand?"

Her room is empty? But where is she?

"Yes," his voice was shaky. "I understand."

I closed my door. More cussing. The bustle of bodies leaving. Then silence.

When they were gone, I quickly crossed the hall. "Leira?" I knocked on her door. No reply. The intruders had left the door unlocked, so I stepped into her room. "Are you in here?" Nothing. No one. The room was empty. On Leira's bed lay the tunic she'd been given by Reyhan the innkeeper.

Obviously this hotel wasn't safe, and I didn't plan on coming back after we were together. I grabbed her tunic and the rest of her things, rushed back to my room and stuffed her things as well as mine into my pack. It wasn't easy, but since we were carrying very little food, I managed. I would find her, and we would leave this city.

I slid my walking stick through an outer strap so I wouldn't have to hold it, then threw open my window, which opened to a terrace overlooking the town. Two stories below me, the fair was in full swing. Tonight they were having a masquerade dance, and everyone, it seemed, was wearing a mask.

Which would only make it harder to find Leira.

I traversed along the edge of the building, crawled down as far as I could, and then dropped into a dark wood. As I stood up and stepped out of the shadows, a figure approached me. At first I thought it might have been Jibben, but then I realized this man was too tall to be him. An instant later I realized it was the hooded man I'd seen earlier on the steps of the temple of Apollyon. He still wore the same flowing cloak.

"Alcion?" I ventured. "Is that you?"

The figure came closer. He shook his head and then spoke with a voice I vaguely recognized. "Kadin," he said. "Come with me."

"Who are you?" I asked.

"A fellow vagabond. I know where Leira is. Follow me."

"What?"

"Hurry!"

I scanned the shadows. No one.

He turned and was moving quickly into the woods.

Without his help you might never find her. Not in this crowd.

At last I began to follow the hooded man into the night, but after only a few steps I regretted my decision. Someone behind a nearby tree coughed, and then, before I realized what was going on, a net dropped onto me. I tried to wrestle free of it, but found myself hopelessly entangled.

Wild laughter and shouting filled the darkness as I struggled to pull free. But the more I moved, the more entwined I became.

A group of ruffians wielding cruelly curved daggers stepped out of the shadows. Some of the men poked torches toward me as if I were a stray dog they'd just caught. The others sneered. While they were mocking me, I recognized the laughter of one of the men. I twisted around so I could see him better.

He nodded to his partners. "We'll be paid well for this one." Then he turned to me and flipped the hood from his head. In the flickering light of the torches I saw the face of the man who had led me into this trap.

Staring at me with a wide grin was Castel.

CHAPTER FOURTEEN

TRAGEDY

"But I thought you were dead!" I gasped as Castel's friends cut through the net. A coachman pulled up with a wagon that held a cage.

Castel laughed, then seized my pack. "What? The archers?"

"Or the wolves. How did you make it here? And why are you helping them?"

"Escaping the archers was easy enough. They were, well, preoccupied with Biminak . . ."

His cold indifference to Biminak's death appalled me. The men had freed me from the net but yanked my arms back to tie my wrists behind my back.

"So then," Castel said, "I was on my own. I found someone who removed the infection on my neck—good thing, too. It was really becoming irritating. And the wolves were getting closer by the day."

The men grabbed my arms and hustled me toward the wagon.

The last time I saw Castel, he hadn't seemed to be bothered by the growth. *The further he traveled in this land, the more it infected it became.* "Where did you get it removed? The inn?"

We were halfway to the caged cart.

He scoffed. "I found a man who specializes in these things." Castel pulled back his cloak to show me his neck. A horribly large, pitted scar stretched from his neck to his shoulder. Whoever had removed his growth had done so with a dagger or a hatchet rather than a dream. "He's the one who told me about Wyckell." Castel leaned close to me with a wicked gleam in his eyes. "And oh, believe me, Kadin, this city is everything they say it is. I'm living proof that you can have both the life of a vagabond and the pleasures of the fair."

"No," I said. "Castel, listen to yourself. They've gotten to you."

By then we'd reached the cage. It was constructed out of thick wooden staves and was only large enough to hold one or two prisoners. With my hands still tied tightly behind my back, the men shoved me into the cage, then clamped shackles around my feet. They chained those to the bars to prevent any chance of escape.

One of the men locked the cage. Behind me I overheard Castel talking to one of his helpers. "Did you find the girl yet?"

"No."

"Well, keep looking. She can't be far. They travel together."

"Castel, don't do this!" I cried. But by then, the coachman had whipped his horses and the wagon jostled forward. "Castel, no!"

But all I heard in reply was the fading sound of his cruel laughter.

◆ ◆ ◆ ◆

Dawn was breaking, but the sky was overcast with slabs of granite-gray clouds. The day seemed impossibly dark, the air itself stained by the sins of this city.

I was caged up like an animal in the center of Wyckell. For all I knew, Leira had been captured as well. And I could only guess what might have happened to Alcion. I wondered if I would see either of them again. If I would ever make it to Celestia at all.

Though it was still early, a crowd was quickly forming. One of the men looked at me and grinned. "Two for the price of one," he said to his friend. Then I remembered that there was another case before the courts today—a traitor who'd been caught yesterday morning. Selfishly, I was happy that at least he might draw some of the attention away from me. But when I noticed the pole looming nearby I couldn't help but shiver.

A few people laughed at me and threw rotten vegetables at my cage. One landed on my lap; another pelted me in the face.

More soldiers were gathering now, and a cluster of them led the prisoner out of a nearby building that I presumed served as their jail. They dragged him toward the steps of the courthouse.

As they moved past me, I saw who the traitor was.

"Alcion!" I cried.

He looked my way. "The strength of Kiral be with you," he said softly. His wrists and ankles were in chains. His shredded shirt hung loosely on his back, and I could tell he'd been whipped.

I was speechless. *Alcion? The traitor?*

No, of course not. Only here in the fair where the rich are poor and those who travel toward freedom are disdained.

Then I remembered the vision Leira had seen and shuddered as I recalled how it ended—with the death of both Alcion and the prince Leira had dreamed about earlier. I wondered if it was possible that I might be the other man in her dream after all.

The crowd had grown larger now. Many of the people still wore their masks from the night before, creating a surreal mixture of real faces and masked identities. Some townspeople jeered; others looked on in silence.

Just then, the door of the courthouse opened, and an enormously fat man with a braided beard appeared. The crowd murmured when they saw him. Two soldiers carried out an ornate throne and set it on a landing at the top of the building's steps. The fat man plopped into it as the soldiers took their positions and stood attentively at his sides.

A nasally sounding knave stepped forward, and the crowd quieted down. "Nawat, Lord of Festivities, Judge of our Land, Magistrate of Wyckell, wishes to speak!" he announced. Then he bowed and retreated backward, into the cluster of officials standing behind the magistrate.

"Who are these men, and what are the charges against them?" Nawat bellowed.

Immediately the crowd erupted into a chorus of accusations and shouts. It was impossible to hear anyone clearly.

Nawat brought a beefy fist down onto the arm of his throne. "Silence!"

The crowd became silent.

"Graylet." Nawat glared at one of his officials. "Who are these men, and why do you interrupt my breakfast to parade them before me!"

"Th-they're tramps, sir." He looked terrified at the prospect of displeasing Nawat. "And disturbers of the peace. They disrupt the business of Wyckell, create unrest and commotion throughout the city, and spread lies about our duly appointed rulers."

Nawat turned to Alcion. "Are these charges true?"

"No, sir."

Back at the outpost Alcion had been shaken by his trip into the Hall of Tales, by his thoughts of this journey to Wyckell, but now, though obviously weak from his beatings, his poise had returned. "I have only spoken of the city of Celestia and encouraged all who would choose the way of the king to make the journey to its gates."

"The way of the king?" Nawat scoffed. "So, you would have the hard-working men and women of Wyckell leave our city to adopt a life of vagrancy and delinquency? What possible good could come of that?"

"I only encourage people to pursue the truth whenever and wherever it—"

"The truth!" Nawat cut in with a sneer. "The truth is I would rather be eating my breakfast than wasting my time talking to you." Ripples of laughter coursed through the crowd.

Graylet, the one who'd pronounced the charges against Alcion, continued, becoming more self-assured when he saw that Nawat's anger was directed at the prisoner rather than at him: "Sir, this man tells the people that the ways of the king of Celestia and the ways of our town are incompatible and can never be reconciled. By saying this he insults our elders, our leaders, our traditions, and our values. His intolerance cannot be accepted. His ideas are treasonous."

"No," Alcion objected. "I have only spoken against those who speak against him who is higher than the highest—King Kiral himself."

"King Kiral himself?!" Nawat spat out the words. "Higher than the highest? He has no authority here. Our master, Baron Dorjan, will be arriving tomorrow. He is our Lord. He is the highest!" The mention of the name of the baron sent a chill down my spine. The crowd murmured their agreement with Nawat.

Then, the fat judge eyed me. "And what of him?"

"This man is just like the other," Castel cried, stepped forward, playing to the crowd. "And he also passes stolen money."

"My money wasn't stolen," I said. "It was—"

"And look what we found in his pack," Castel went on, undaunted. He held up the tooth of Apollyon that Leira had wrenched from the beast's mouth. The crowd gasped. Some of the people dropped to the ground face-first and started muttering prayers and incantations to their fallen god.

"He has slain Apollyon, our great god and protector!" Castel shouted. "He is a wizard of dark magik!"

Frightened whispers scampered through the crowd:

"Murderer . . ."

"Wizard . . ."

"Burn the heretic!"

"He has attacked our god!"

"He desecrates our land!"

Nawat's face was growing red as his anger against me sharpened.

Castel looked like he was about to go on, but before he could, a wizened old man dressed in a flowing pale orange robe stepped forward and raised his decorative staff to silence the crowd. As he cleared his throat, everyone quieted down. He spoke softly, but no one moved when he addressed the magistrate.

"Your Honor and Glory," he said with a bow, "as you know I am Samein, servant of Dorjan, priest of the temple of Apollyon, humble slave of your judgeship."

His words were welcomed with nods from the crowd. Nawat the magistrate nodded as well.

Samein continued, "This man has attacked our city's most ancient and revered god, Apollyon—"

"Apollyon is dead!" wailed someone from the crowd.

But the old priest shook his head firmly. "Not dead, friends. Insulted. Angered. You read these signs wrong. You cannot kill Apollyon. This man only found the tooth of our great god in the corpse of a rotting heretic he saw fit to eat."

"No, I killed him," I whispered under my breath. Why was he saying those things? Why was he lying?

Then immediately I realized that the dragon had been this man's god and he couldn't accept that his faith, his career, his entire life, was a charade, that his god was really dead, that all he'd believed in, worked for, was a lie.

Nawat the magistrate nodded and, with a considerable amount of effort, stood up. "It's clear that these men teach sedition, attack our way of life, and desire nothing more than the downfall of our great city and our gods. Here is the sentence the gods have revealed to me—death! Today we burn the old man, tomorrow the boy!"

The crowd cheered. Some began to chant, "Death! Death! Death!" A riot was forming. Nawat raised both hands to calm the crowd. After a few moments, everyone was quiet again. Then he turned to Castel, who'd been cheering along with the rest of the townspeople. "You were once a vagabond too?" he said coolly.

"Yes, your honor. Long ago. That's why I've helped your men capture these two. For I know their trickery well. I know all about—"

The lord of the fair spat on the ground, stopping Castel in mid-sentence. "If you are so helpful, Castel, why does the girl still elude us?"

"The girl?" Castel sputtered.

"I'm not stupid, you fool. I know vagabonds travel together. I know how many have entered our city this week."

My heart sank. I'd been hoping maybe they would forget about Leira. But they had not. Now she would be in as much danger as I was.

Castel swallowed hard. "We'll find her, sir," he said. "It's just a matter of time."

The magistrate narrowed his eyes at Castel. "Yes, we will find her, or *you* will take her place at the stake tomorrow with the boy."

Then he raised his scepter and pointed it toward Alcion. "Burn him!"

"Burn him!" the crowd cried together, almost as one.

No!

Nawat calmed down the crowd one last time and then looked at Alcion disdainfully. "So that none can accuse us of injustice or rash judgment, we will give the convict a chance to respond to the charges."

Alcion stared at the lord of the fair for a long moment without saying a word.

"Well? Do you wish to speak or not, old man?"

Alcion licked his parched and split lips. "We have something in common, sir."

Nawat looked at him disdainfully. "What is that?"

"Neither of us is afraid of the other. I am not afraid to die for the truth, and you are not afraid to kill for a lie."

Nawat's face turned crimson with rage. "Burn him!" he screamed, his fat jowls shaking. "Now. In front of me!"

"No!" I yelled.

One of the guards smacked me in the face with my own walking stick, which had been brought to my cage. "Quiet!" he sneered. He hit me three more times, knocking me nearly unconscious before throwing the walking stick down beside the wagon. Reeling in pain, I stared between the bars. The guard leaned close enough for me to smell his wretched breath. "We'll use that stick as kindling tomorrow when it's your turn." He grinned and then turned to watch the execution of Alcion.

I began to shake.

This can't be happening!

They led Alcion to the wooden post anchored securely in the ground at the center of the fair. One of the guards clamped Alcion's wrists into the post's rusty shackles above his head.

No! No! No!

A guard with a long scar snaking down his right cheek piled more dry sticks around his legs.

"This is how we treat our criminals," he said to Alcion. As he backed away from Alcion, he sneered, "I enjoy seeing people like you die."

Alcion looked at him concernedly. "And I enjoy seeing people like you live."

For just a moment, the guard paused and studied the face of this condemned man. Something passed between them. Alcion nodded, smiling faintly. "Soon," he said. "Soon."

When the scarred guard hesitated, the soldier beside him snatched a torch from the hands of one of the townspeople and lowered it toward the stack of wood.

"No!" I screamed. But my voice was swallowed in the chorus of cheers from the excited crowd.

I couldn't watch. I shut my eyes.

The crackle of the fire blazed louder, along with the soft voice of Alcion singing the song he had learned in the courtyard of the king—the same tune I'd heard so many times in the glowing halls of the outpost while the three sisters who never grew old copied the ancient tales.

But now, at last, Alcion sang the words.

The roar of the blaze became filled with his song, and the people who'd been cheering to see him die hushed into silence.

I opened my eyes at that point, not to watch Alcion, but to

watch the crowd. Many people had turned away and lowered their heads. To my shock, a few of them crying. I could only guess that they weren't used to seeing their criminals die like that, with dignity and without fear. "What kind of man is this?" I heard someone nearby whisper. "Who sings in the flames?"

The song became fainter as the fire blazed higher.

The guard with the long scar snaking down his cheek just stood staring at the burning stake.

Eventually the singing stopped and the people began to walk away. The fire burned out. It was all over.

Alcion was dead.

"Tomorrow you'll join him," hissed the soldier who stood beside my cage.

That day I expected to be mocked and perhaps even beaten periodically, but the people in Wyckell gave me a wide berth. Even the ones in charge of setting up a new pole looked uneasy and hurried off as soon as they'd completed their task. After watching Alcion die, the people seemed to be afraid of me.

That night, only one guard was stationed to watch me.

My hands were still tied behind my back, so when it became dark, I leaned my back against the bars and tried once again to loosen them, but they wouldn't budge.

I knew that in the morning I would be put to death, burned just as Alcion had been, yet strangely, I was filled more with concern than with fear. All I could think of was Leira and what might have happened to her. I knew it was too late for me. I could only hope it wasn't too late for her. Maybe, just maybe, she'd made it out of the city.

Just after the moon rose, a woman came strolling along the street toward my cage. Apparently, all the other partygoers in Wyckell had decided they would rather not party near the condemned wizard who had attacked and possibly killed their god.

As she came closer, the soldier watched her intently.

"Hello," she called to him.

"Hello." He was becoming more interested in her the closer she came.

The woman wore a leopard's mask and moved like a cat. She sauntered closer. "I was just looking for someone to have some fun with," she pouted. "You look busy, but no one else is around tonight." She'd reached his side by then and trailed a finger along his chin. "Would you like to have a little fun with a lonely girl?"

He poked his thumb toward me. "On duty." He didn't sound very convinced of the fact.

"Of course," she said coyly. "I understand." Then she got really close to his ear. "Maybe another time then. But I was really hoping for some company *tonight*."

She turned and started to walk away but only made it half a dozen paces before he called to her. "Wait!" He yanked at the bars a couple times to assure himself that I wasn't going anywhere, smirked at me, and then followed her toward a wooded area nearby.

A moment after the two of them had disappeared into the shadows I heard a loud smack, a gasp, and then a muffled thud.

My heart began beating faster as three figures emerged from the shadows where only two had entered. The girl had been a decoy probably, just to lure the soldier away to rob him. Now as she left the woods, she was accompanied by two men; one was quite large.

As the three figures stepped into the moonlight, the girl spoke. "This makes two times I've saved your life, Kadin. Not that anyone's keeping track, of course."

And with that, Leira peeled off her leopard mask and reached for her hairpin.

CHAPTER FIFTEEN

Dark River

The three of them hurried to my cage. I immediately recognized the smaller man. "Jibben? What are you doing here!"

He bowed low. "I told you I was here to serve you."

"He betrayed us!" I told Leira.

"No, Kadin." She was slipping her hairpin into the cage's lock. "He was trying to help us all along. He's the one who found me in the crowd and kept me hidden all day."

I didn't know what to think. "But how? In all the masks?"

"The bracelet she wore on her left wrist," Jibben explained. "The one she bought yesterday. It's from the silver mines of Demas. Very rare. I searched the entire city until I found her."

Earlier, I'd convinced myself that Jibben had disclosed our whereabouts, so now I could hardly believe he was helping us. But I was even more shocked when I saw the face of my final rescuer. "You?" It was the guard with the long scar on his cheek. "You're helping us?"

"He has become a vagabond," Leira blurted before the man could answer.

I eyed him skeptically. "Is that true?"

He nodded. "Those words your friend spoke to me at his death: 'I enjoy seeing people like you live.' I wondered how a condemned man could talk like that. I knew Jibben worked with the vagabonds who traveled through Wyckell, so I asked him about it. He told me about the Book of Blood and the city of Celestia and a land ruled by something even stronger than magik."

I said nothing. I was still too stunned.

The guard found his keys and unclasped the shackles around my ankles, but Leira was still working at the cage's lock—apparently he didn't have a key to that.

"He's leaving Wyckell," Leira explained.

"Are you coming with us tonight?" I asked the guard.

He shook his head. "I have family here. I'm going to try to convince them to come too. I have to. I love them."

I nodded. I understood that feeling completely.

The lock finally popped open.

"How do you do that?" I asked Leira in amazement.

She slipped her hairpin back into her hair. "I told you, I'm good with locks."

I wanted to ask Leira to explain what had happened—what had changed her mind from being so enticed by the city to coming to help me, but it didn't seem like the right time for the question.

Jibben untied my hands, and the guard handed us our packs, which he'd retrieved from the magistrate's storage room earlier in the evening. "You have to go on foot through the woods," he directed us. "Your horses would attract too much attention."

"Don't worry," Jibben said. "They're all taken care of. I'll be returning them to the outpost."

"Be gentle with the brown one," I said. "She's a little sensitive."

Jibben looked at me and then at Leira. "But they're both stallions . . ."

"What does that mean?" I asked.

"It means they're both boy horses," Leira said. "I didn't have the heart to tell you before. You were so convinced your horse could hear you and kept referring to him as a girl."

"Oh," I muttered. "I see."

The guard handed me my walking stick, we thanked him and Jibben, and then Leira and I headed into the night.

"The strength of Kiral be with you," Jibben called to us in a hushed but urgent voice.

"And with you as well," we said together.

Leira and I snuck around the edge of a small lake nestled in the woods. As we slipped away, she threw off the jewelry she'd purchased at the fair. The silver bracelet landed in the middle of the lake where it sank out of sight with a soft splash.

"Good riddance," she said, making me even more curious about her change of attitude from just last night.

We skirted along the trail through the forest, checking to make sure we weren't being followed. When we were several miles from the city and seemed to be out of immediate danger, I asked her if she'd seen what happened to Alcion.

She nodded sadly.

"I can't believe he's gone," I said.

"I know."

"So where were you? What happened to you in Wyckell?"

Leira took a long, sad breath. "Kadin, I'm so sorry. After I left you, I lay in bed trying to sleep but all I could think of was the fair. Finally, I got up and slipped out. I bought a mask and joined the festivities."

She paused for a moment before going on. "The dancing, the jewelry, the people—they helped me forget."

"Forget?"

"My bruises," she said softly.

I was silent then for a long time. I couldn't think of anything to say.

She sighed sadly. "When Alcion was killed, it was like everything finally became clear. The fair—how foolish I'd been. I was so ashamed. That is a city that kills vagabonds. They were going to kill you, kill me. But still, I was ready to *stay* there! I can hardly believe it."

Still unsure what to say, I finally just reached for her hand. And for the first time since we'd walked through the dark pit, we held hands. And we ran together through the night.

◆ ◆ ◆ ◆

The next morning, with the help of the map, we found the king's pathway and continued on our journey toward the land of the ancient kings and the city of Celestia.

Those days following the death of Alcion were the saddest of my life. There were so many things I'd wanted to ask him, to tell him. I wished I'd taken better advantage of our brief time together, but it was too late for that now. It was too late for anything.

One morning, Leira must have noticed how distraught I was feeling. "There's nothing you can do about it, Kadin," she said to me on the second day. "We just have to believe he's at peace now."

"Do you believe that?"

She didn't think about it long. "Yes. I do."

I had no idea what it would feel like to have a faith that strong. I wondered if I had any faith at all.

"Last night," she said, "I dreamt of him. Of Alcion."

"You did! What did you see? What happened?"

"My dream picked up where the vision in the Hall of Tales ended. After I saw the face of the second man, I heard a noise and turned to see a carriage stop nearby. The king himself stepped out and went over to Alcion's body. He took him by the hand and helped him to his feet—and he wasn't dead, Kadin. In my dream, Alcion wasn't dead! The king led him to the carriage. Then Alcion turned to me. 'Soon,' he said. 'Soon.' And then they rode off together, laughing."

That's the same thing Alcion had said to the guard right before his execution.

"Laughing? They were laughing that you would soon be, what . . . dead?"

"No, it wasn't that. It was something else, though I don't exactly know what. The other man, the prince, stirred and stood beside me and took my hand. Then, my dream ended, and when I awoke, I was filled with fear, but also with hope."

I was silent. *Fear and hope.*

Every night from then on I wished a dream could come to me that offered me a little less of the first and a little more of the second.

But no dreams came.

◆ ◆ ◆ ◆

In the days that followed, Leira and I spent lots of time reading from the Book of Blood. It seemed like a good way to honor Alcion. And it did help ease the pain of losing him, at least a little. The words of the book reminded me why I'd become a vagabond in the first place and where Alcion had gone after his death—to a brighter and better world.

That is, if the words in the book were true. Sometimes I doubted them, sometimes I believed them. It was a hard place to be, lost somewhere between faith and uncertainty.

One day Leira and I came to a field covered with beautiful purple and ivory flowers.

"This field, these flowers," I said. "I know where we are."

She looked around uneasily. "The enchanted ground."

I nodded.

Asvina had told us of this place one night at the castle. Long ago, before he was slain by the prince, this land had been cursed by Killius, the dark wizard. According to legend, the aromatic flowers and the warmth of the sun worked together to cause travelers to become sleepy. As Asvina had explained, "Some people say that those who sleep there never awaken, others say that a witch finds them and makes them her slaves. However, the path to Celestia cuts straight through the field. All vagabonds must cross it."

Leira and I entered the enchanted ground and I said, "We have to stay awake. No matter how tired we may get, we can't stop walking."

A nod.

We walked for some time and I truly did find myself getting sleepy. Hoping it would keep us both awake, I suggested we talk.

"What do you want to talk about?" Leira asked.

"I don't know. Girls always want to talk. This is your chance. What do *you* want to talk about?"

She was quiet for a moment. "I don't know. I can't think of anything."

"Neither can I."

"You sure?"

"Pretty sure."

For a moment we traveled quietly, and I wondered how far we could make it by just discussing what we might talk about. Finally she said, "How about I tell you about my dream, the one in which my neck was healed?"

"Perfect."

"I dreamt I was standing outside a castle. A great dance was about to begin inside, but I hadn't been allowed in because I wasn't royalty. Instead, I'd been assigned to take care of the horses in the stable. That was okay with me, but all at once when the music started, a servant came rushing outside with a parchment in his hand—an invitation from the prince himself. 'Come on,' the servant said. 'Hurry, he's waiting.' But then he noticed my clothes. 'Oh, you mustn't appear before the prince in those!' He took me to a room filled with the finest dresses in the world and told me to choose one that I liked."

I thought back to the day when I'd come upon Leira trying on Shika's dress, and how surprised I'd been that she didn't consider herself pretty.

She went on, "Well, in my dream I chose a silk dress. It was stunning. Truly gorgeous. And when I slipped it on, it fit perfectly. But when I turned to the mirror to see how I looked, my face was covered with bruises again, just like before. Then the servant returned and told me the prince was waiting. 'No!' I cried. 'I could never let him see me like this!' I began to weep and refused to leave the room."

We walked a few steps in silence.

"Finally the servant left, and I was about to change into my old clothes and return to my work in the stables when I heard a key in the lock. The door swung open and standing there before me was the prince himself. 'I called for you and you wouldn't come,' he said. 'Why not?' I covered my face with my hands and crumpled to the floor, ashamed. 'Your Majesty,' I whispered, 'I couldn't come, not when I look like this.' I thought he might leave, or perhaps punish me for wasting his time, but then I felt his hand on my shoulder. He helped me to my feet, and when I looked at him he brushed the hair and tears out of my eyes and said, 'I see only beauty.'"

She paused as if to collect her thoughts. "I didn't know what to say to him. I looked past him into the mirror and gasped. The bruises were gone. My face had been transformed. I looked—"

"Like a princess," I offered.

Leira glanced at me strangely. "Yes."

"Lucky guess."

"Well, the prince leaned close and whispered into my ear, 'I've been waiting a long time for this dance. Don't make me wait any longer.' He took my hand and led me into the hallway and we danced to the music. As the song ended, people parted, and I saw the king himself, seated on a throne. I curtsied. And then he said two words to me—just two words."

"What were they?"

"'Welcome, daughter.' And that's when I awoke."

We walked for a few moments in silence, and I found myself getting more and more drowsy. "Say something, Leira." I yawned. "I'm getting sleepier."

She yawned back at me. "It's your turn. Tell me about your dream."

And I did. I told her all about the tree and the cave and the branch. Then we talked about our old lives in Abaddon and our emerging dreams of the future—and though we were both weary and sleepy, our stories kept us alert, kept us awake.

Kept us alive.

As the sun was setting, we left the field of enchanted flowers and arrived at a fertile valley filled with fruit trees surrounding a small lake. Lush hills rose around us, creating a sheltered alcove for the orchard. The mountains, once so distant against the horizon, had become closer and looked more majestic than ever.

After checking the book and confirming that the fruit wasn't poisonous, we ate some, and then—as twilight fell and night embraced us—lay down to sleep.

In the morning when we were getting packed I couldn't find the Book of Blood. "Leira, do you have the book?"

"No. Why?"

"It's gone." I scanned the campsite. Nothing.

"Did you leave it somewhere again?" she asked icily.

"We had it last night before we went to bed—remember?" I studied the ground again. "Wait." This time I saw something. I pointed. "Footprints." Leading away from our campfire and up one of the nearby hills were fresh boot prints in the moist soil. "Come on."

We ran up the hill. From the summit, we could see a broad and dark river winding out of sight toward the horizon. Its water was the color of midnight, and the current was swift and swollen with recently melted snow. Morning mist circled above it, curling up toward the rising sun.

"The river that has no bridge," Leira whispered. "I didn't know we'd made it this far." Indeed we'd read that all vagabonds must cross the bridgeless river that flows along the border of the land of the ancient kings.

At the river's edge was a ferryboat. A ferryman whom I didn't know stood inside it. Another man stood onshore. I recognized him immediately.

"Castel!" I felt a deep surge of anger.

Turning abruptly, Castel saw us and stepped aboard the boat. In his hand was the Book of Blood—*my* Book of Blood. He spoke in a hushed voice to the ferryman who pushed away from the riverbank as Leira and I raced down the hill toward them. But by the time we'd reached the shore, Castel and the ferry were already thirty or forty feet from shore.

Castel smiled smugly. "Always one step behind, aren't you?"

"What are you doing?"

"Why, going to Celestia!" He laughed, but it was dark

laughter soaked with derision. Any joy that used to live in his heart must have drained away during his stay in Wyckell. He pointed a long bony finger at Leira. "When I heard they wanted to burn me in place of her, I thought it might be a good time to resume my journey. I knew the general direction, and of course, when I found that tooth in your pack I'd noticed your book of maps. I kept the news to myself at the time, thinking I could steal it later and sell it. But then when you escaped and I saw you two walking through that field of flowers, I followed you, and, well . . . here we are."

Fog began to curl toward them. As the boat turned into the current, I could see part of its name written in bold letters across the bow, but only a few of the letters were visible: *The Ki—*

"Castel, listen to me. You can't take a ferry across this river," I warned. "And you can't cross the river here. It's too far to—"

"You're just trying to trick me to get your book back," he retorted. "I'll be okay. After all, I've got this, don't I?" He patted the Book of Blood. "I told you I could have the best of both worlds, Kadin."

The ferryman, dressed in a black robe, remained quiet as the fog, which thickened in the middle of the river, began to engulf them.

"We're serious Castel," yelled Leira. "The book warns against it. You have to cross the river yourself, with no boat. And you don't have a pardon!"

But Castel would not be dissuaded. He'd settled onto one of the ferry's seats and opened up the Book of Blood. "Now, let's see where we go from here."

Leira and I hurried along the riverbank to stay as close as possible to them as they floated downstream.

The boatman poled them into the deeper, swifter water, then turned and looked at us. His flesh was stretched tightly across his face like a skintight mask, but beneath the skin, something else moved. Something that was not human. I'd seen that horrible expression before, in the dark pit beyond Apollyon's lair. Now, the ferryman curled back his lips and opened his mouth. His jaw unhinged like that of a snake, making his mouth big enough to bite off a human head.

"Castel!" I yelled. "Jump! Get out of the boat now! The ferryman! Watch out for the ferryman!"

Just then the boat turned enough for me to read the bow: *The Killius.*

"Hurry, Castel!" I hollered. "Jump!"

Then the mists swallowed them. I heard Castel laugh for a moment—but only for moment. His sour laughter quickly turned into something else. A cry of terror echoed across the water and then a choked scream chilled the morning air.

Then all was quiet except for the sound of the river lapping hungrily at our feet.

Neither of us said anything for a long time.

"The current is so strong," she whispered at last. "How could anyone get across? How could anyone survive?"

"I asked the sisters at the castle the same question," I said, "after reading about this river in the Book of Blood."

"What did they say?"

I took a deep breath. "They told me no one does."

"What?"

"No one survives."

"Oh," she muttered. "I see."

Leira turned away from the mists swirling above the swift, dark water and I followed her back to our campsite, hoping we could still find the right pathway to Celestia without our maps.

◆ ◆ ◆ ◆

Thankfully, the trail that led past the fruit trees was easy to follow for most of the day. We were confident it was the correct trail because, although rocky, it headed straight toward the eastern horizon.

Eventually it split into two parallel trails—one strewn with rocks, the other; which lay just on the other side of a crumbling stone wall, looked smooth and easy.

I climbed to the top of the tumbled boulders that had at one time been a wall and scouted out both pathways. As far as I could see, they continued side by side with only the ancient stone wall separating them.

I heard thunder rumble somewhere in the distance. "Leira, let's take the path here, on the left. It's not as rocky. I think we can make better time—maybe even outrun that storm."

She studied the two paths suspiciously. "That one seems to veer off from the trail."

It didn't look that much different to me. "I don't think it matters which one we take. They parallel each other. This one will be faster." I heard the thunder again. "It sounds like we're in for quite a storm, and it looks like there's a forest up ahead on this side of the wall. Lots more shelter."

"I don't know, Kadin. What if the trail heads off in another direction?"

I scanned the two trails again, comparing them carefully. "If it starts to, we'll just climb back over the wall. Come on. Let's get going. Before the rain starts."

At last I convinced her. She scrambled over the rocks to join me. We hadn't gone far before we heard someone approaching from behind. Turning around I saw that it was a woman dressed in a tunic similar to the one Leira wore. She was traveling alone and hurrying up the trail.

"Vagabonds?" she called. "Are you vagabonds?"

"Yes," I said, convinced by her clothes that at the moment honesty was the best route to take.

"I've come from the palace of Gaius and the three sisters," she cried. "I just made it through Wyckell. Oh, poor Alcion! I heard of him, everyone did. The whole fair is talking about him."

"She's one of us," Leira said.

I asked the woman, who was now only thirty paces away,

"Is this the way to the city? Do you know?"

"Yes." She was nearly out of breath. "To Celestia."

"Are you sure?" Leira asked.

"It's smooth and straight," she said, as if that was the answer.

She arrived, kept walking; we had to hustle to keep up with her. "Just up ahead, just past the forest, that's where we cross the river. That's where it's the shallowest."

"But do you have a map?" Leira asked her.

The woman looked confused. "My husband does, have you seen him?" We both shook our heads no.

"Well, he must be up ahead somewhere." She looked around nervously. "We were trying to outrun the storm." She picked up her pace even more. "I'll meet you two at the river. On to Celestia!"

Clearly, she was not interested in traveling with us.

"The strength of Kiral be with you," I said.

"Yes, yes," she called back. "And with you as well."

I wondered why her husband wasn't with her, but before I could ask her about it, she was gone, rushing on ahead of us. We followed her for about a mile, but then lost sight of her as dusk closed in and she entered the forest.

"She said this path was smooth and straight," Leira said.

"It is," I replied.

"But just because it's easier doesn't mean it's the right one."

I wasn't sure what to say. Thunder rumbled again, closer this time. The wind began whipping up. "Let's look for some shelter. To sit out the storm."

We searched the tree line for anything that might provide protection. The forest that had looked so promising was filled with tall birch trees that swayed wildly in the wind. A few branches, and then an entire tree, crashed to the ground nearby.

"I'm not going in there," Leira said.

But the farther we went up the trail, the fiercer the storm became. Thin streaks of lightning splintered the darkened day, and sheets of rain began to fall.

I thought maybe we could get back to the path on the other side of the wall, but when I climbed up to look for it, it was nowhere in sight.

"Is it there?" Leira asked anxiously.

"No."

That's when I heard the scream from somewhere ahead of us in the trees.

"Did you heard that?" Leira gasped.

"It's the woman we met," I cried. "Come on!" We dashed up the trail.

The clouds had blotted out almost all of the remaining daylight, and the path was shrouded with the coming night. Suddenly, in a flash of lightning, I saw a great hole gaping open in the middle of the path. "Leira, stop!"

I threw my arm out and caught her just in time. Lightning crinkled through the sky, and now she saw the hole and drew back toward me. A manmade pit had been covered with a thin layer of sticks and leaves—gone, now that the woman had crashed through it. In another slash of lightening I saw that at the bottom of the pit, a tangle of sharp spears stuck up toward us. Our fellow vagabond's body lay impaled at the bottom of the dark pit.

"No!" Leira cowered back from the edge. Yellow lightning flashed around us, and the wild sky raged overhead. "I knew we should have stayed on the trail!"

"I'm sorry. I thought—"

"That's the problem!" Leira was becoming hysterical. "You *thought*. You didn't *trust the trail*. That's been your problem all along."

"But this way looked safe to—"

Thunder boomed in my ears. A bolt of lightning ripped across the sky, sending a tree careening into the side of a nearby hill.

Leira was shaking now. "You only trust what you see. You only trust yourself, Kadin."

Her words stung. I tried to think of something to say to refute her, some way to argue back, to prove her wrong, but there was nothing I could say. She was right. So many of the problems I'd gotten myself—and her—into on this journey had come because I'd been careless or trusted my eyes instead of the trail.

"Yes," I told her. "You're right." Rainwater had drenched us by then. The storm swirled all around us in the darkened sky. "I'm sorry, Leira. In the morning we'll backtrack. We'll get on the other path again. I promise. But right now we need to find some shelter."

She was silent. For a moment I thought she might say something like, "*We* aren't going anywhere; *I'm* going on by myself." But she didn't.

She just started crying. "Hold me."

I wrapped my arms around her trembling body. I knew it was the closest she had ever come to saying, "I forgive you."

Yet it was close enough for me.

◆ ◆ ◆ ◆

When the tree nearby had fallen, it'd pulled up its root system creating a hole in the earth just big enough for the two of us to hide in to get out of the storm We huddled there together, hoping no more trees would fall around—or on top of—us.

We dried off as much as possible and then eventually fell asleep.

That night, my dreams were not pleasant ones. I dreamt that I was in a river, fighting to stay afloat, but something was dragging me under. I gasped for breath and tried to swim to shore, but the current was too strong. Then in my terror I saw a body floating in the water ahead of me, the body of a drowned woman. And I heard a voice repeating over and over, "Killius lives . . . Killius lives." Struggling to stay afloat, I ended up swallowing a mouthful of water and slipping beneath the surface one final time.

That's when I woke up shaking.

The sunlight on the ground told me the storm had passed. Birds chirped busily at each other in the trees around us. Beneath me, the ground trembled slightly.

I sat up.

Leira was still asleep. Reyhan had told me to look out for her, but so much of the time it was Leira who'd been looking out for—

The ground trembled again, causing her to stir slightly.

Just then a dark shadow blotted out the sun, but it made me uneasy because, when I looked out the opening of our small earthen shelter, I didn't see any clouds.

Another tremor shook us, this one even closer. As it did, Leira opened her eyes. "What was that?" she asked, still half-asleep.

But she didn't stay half-asleep for long. A voice as loud as last night's storm thundered all around us: "Who dares trespass on my land!"

We peered out the opening, only to see the feet and hairy legs of a man, but not a man like any I'd ever seen. His feet were nearly as long as I was tall. The giant towered above us, the size of nine or ten normal men.

"Thieves! Trespassers!" he roared, then slammed a spiked cudgel against the ground, sending clods of loose dirt raining down on our heads. He threw the club into the woods, reached into our hiding place, then picked up Leira in his left hand and me in his right, as if we were dolls. His arms were as sturdy as tree trunks.

The giant lifted us toward his huge misshapen face, closed his eyes, and sniffed us. Then he grinned and said one final word: "Dinner."

CHAPTER SIXTEEN

DESPAIR

According to the Book of Blood, this giant—named Maul—had been originally stationed here by the evil wizard Killius to stop traders from entering Celestia. Maul was the last sentry along the border.

He carried us toward an enormous castle that had been built on a high cliff. The dark river slithered along the base of the cliff like a rippling snake. On the other side of the river I glimpsed the high, mist-enshrouded walls of a glittering city.

"Celestia," I exclaimed.

Leira said nothing.

With the two of us in his hands, Maul leaned his back against a door to open it, stomped down a flight of enormous stairs, opened another door, and pitched us into his dungeon.

We tumbled across the hard-packed dirt floor.

"The baron will be happy I found you," he grunted. Apparently, on the way to his castle he'd decided that we would serve him better as a bribe than as a meal. "He'll give me enough meat for a month."

We watched the prison door slam shut, sending a cloud of dust fluttering into the air.

"We have to get out of here." I leapt to my feet to search for a means of escape. But when I turned toward Leira I saw her curled up motionlessly on the ground. "Leira! Are you okay?"

She didn't respond.

I ran to her. "Are you hurt? Leira? What's wrong?"

"What's *wrong!*" she cried. "What's *right?* First we take the wrong trail; then we get caught by a giant. And now—did you hear that? The baron is coming here. He's going to take me back."

"I won't let that happen. I promise." I scanned the walls. "I'm going to get you out of here."

I saw a tear on her cheek. "I wish I were back home."

She had lived in Abaddon, but it had never been home to her, not really. I searched for what to say. "Home is where we're going. Celestia. Trust me. We'll get there. We will."

Leira looked at me quizzically. I reached over to dry her tears, but she pulled away. "Kadin, we aren't going anywhere. The book says no one has ever escaped Maul's dungeon."

I was hoping she wouldn't remember that part. "No one has *yet*."

But she shook her head. "You heard what they said in Wyckell—the baron was going to arrive the day after we left. If he's riding on horseback, he could get here any time."

"Then we need to hurry, don't we?" I was doing my best to sound optimistic, hoping it would help, but at first glance, I couldn't see any way out of this dungeon.

Her tears stopped. Then Leira's voice became oddly cool, resigned in a way that frightened me. "Remember when we were at Apollyon's cave and you promised to do anything to keep me from being taken back to the baron's dungeon?"

Her words were making me more and more uneasy. "Yes."

"I need you to do it."

"What are you talking about?"

"Kadin, you know what I mean. If you don't do it, I will."

"Listen, to what you're saying. We've made it this far. We'll get out—I don't know how, but we will. I promise."

"Do you really believe that?"

"Yes, I do."

"Really?"

I hesitated for a moment, weighing the importance of my words. Did I believe, or was I just trying to tell her something to put her hope in? That really was the question. That had been the question for a long time.

Brushing away her tears, I looked her in her eyes. "Yes, really. I do. Come on; stand up." I held out my hand for her. "You wouldn't want to let down your prince, would you? He's been waiting a long time for his dance."

She looked at me then as if she were seeing me for the very first time. I wasn't sure she would take my hand, but finally she did.

"Okay," she said softly.

"Come on." I helped her to her feet. "Let's find a way out of this dungeon."

◆ ◆ ◆ ◆

That day, we searched the cell inch by inch, trying to find a loose stone, a hidden trap door, anything.

All to no avail.

"There's always a secret passageway in these dungeons," I said, trying to raise her spirits. "You read about them all the time in books."

Unfortunately, the person who'd designed Maul's dungeon hadn't read those books. The room appeared to be escape-proof.

The ceiling of our cell was a full fifty feet above us. The only light came from a single window with thick bars about three-quarters of the way up the wall. Even though the room was large enough to hold a giant, the window itself was human-sized. But any hopes of sliding between the bars of the window were dashed when I saw how closely together they were positioned.

At least we weren't chained up and were able to move around. That was good.

The walls of the dungeon were slick from water that seeped between the stones and made them too slippery to climb. That was bad, because the only other opening besides the window was the huge door Maul had used to access the dungeon. And even if it were unlocked, it appeared far too heavy for us to budge.

In several places, dark stains lurked on the walls. I didn't really want to know what the stains were from, but since they were near rusty shackles I was pretty sure I knew.

The day after he stuck us in the dungeon, Maul returned. "Here," he hollered, throwing our packs and my walking stick into the cell. Then he slammed the door with an enormous thud. He was laughing as he walked away.

"Hmm," I said, "maybe he's not such a bad guy after all." I promptly opened up my pack in search of something to eat, but discovered he'd taken out all of our food. "I take that back."

"At least he doesn't want us to die quickly," Leira said wryly, holding up a full wineskin of water.

"Well, that's something."

Throughout the day, we took advantage of Maul's absence and searched the cell again and again for any means of escape. But each time we came up empty. We knew Baron Dorjan could arrive at any time, and when he did, we would be beaten, tortured, and perhaps even fed to the giant. And there wasn't much we could do about it, unless of course, we could find a way out first.

At night, after Leira had fallen asleep, I stared out the window of the cell and watched the stars. Black strips of starless sky told me where each prison bar was located. Somehow . . . somehow . . . we would get out. *I know it. I believe it . . .*

The next morning, convinced that there were no secret tunnels or hidden passageways, we took inventory of what we had: two wineskins of water, one half-empty flask of healing water from the inn, a few grimy clothes, the coil of the one hundred or so feet of rope the shepherd had given me, a walking stick, and a hairpin.

As I looked over the pile of objects, my eyes landed on the hairpin. I looked up at the dungeon's door. "Leira, maybe you could pick that lock. After all, you've done it before."

She stared at the door's lock, at least twenty feet above us. "How would I even get up there?"

"I could give you a boost."

She shook her head. "Kadin, even if you were fifteen feet tall and I was somehow able to reach the handle and unlock the door what good would it do? We could never push that door open to get away. It's too heavy."

"Well, I'm open to suggestions."

She studied the walls of the dungeon once again and at last she shook her head and sighed. "Okay, I guess it's worth a try."

At first I tried holding her on my shoulders. She was right; it wasn't even close to the elusive lock. After I lowered her to the ground, I remembered the rope and snatched it up. "Maybe if I can throw one end of this over the handle of the door, you can climb it to the lock."

Leira looked at me skeptically.

I took off my left boot and tied one end of the rope to it to give me some weight to throw. My first three tosses weren't even close. But then on the fourth try, the boot hit the top of the handle and tipped to the other side, allowing the rope to straddle it. It took only a few gentle flicks of the rope to lower the boot to the ground.

"All right." I untied the boot. "Let's give this a shot."

Leira stared at the rope. "Okay, tell me again how this is going to work? You expect me to climb that?"

"You don't have to climb it. I'll tie a loop in one end, we'll thread it under your armpits and I'll hoist you up." I began to tie a loop and made sure it wouldn't tighten when pressure was put on the rope.

She shook her head. "Kadin, I think I might weigh more than you think I do."

From all the hiking she was slim. I knew I could do it. "I can lift you. Trust me."

First we tried looping the rope under her armpits, but when she suggested she might slip out of it if she raised her hands, I lowered it to her ribs, then grabbed some extra clothing and stuffed it under the rope as padding.

"Kadin, you won't be able to hold me."

"Sure I will." I wrapped the rope several times around my waist, tightened it up. "Once you pick the lock we'll figure out a way to swing the door open."

She still didn't seem convinced. I wound the rope around

my wrists and backed up, bringing the rope taut. "Here goes."

Honestly, I wasn't sure I'd be able to hoist her up, but she must have weighed even less than I thought, and all those days on the trail had strengthened my muscles.

It was actually working.

The further I backed up, the more she rose until she was at the lock. She held on with one hand, taking some of the pressure off the rope, and I leaned back and locked myself in position.

With her free hand she maneuvered her hairpin expertly into the lock to coax it open.

Nothing.

After a while she sighed and shook her head. "Kadin, I can't do it. The lock is too big for a hairpin. It's giant-sized."

"Try again!"

She did, but got nowhere. "I can't do it, Kadin. The rope is starting to hurt."

"Just try once more."

"The lock is too big, we have to try someth—"

I heard Maul stomping down the steps to our cell. "It's him!"

She let go of the lock and I moved toward her, trying to lower her quickly, while also trying to keep her from smacking onto the ground.

By the sound of it, the giant was only a few steps away.

She landed, freed herself from the rope, then tossed the clothes we'd used as padding toward our packs.

"The rope," she mouthed.

I yanked the rope toward me as the door began to open. The rope sailed through the air and sprawled across the ground at my feet.

Desperately, I shoved it into the shadowy recesses of the dungeon.

The giant entered, and Leira rushed toward him, her hands to her face. "I've had enough!" Whether she was acting or not, she sounded like she was crying. "Kill me now. Please, before the baron comes!"

What? She can't be—

Maul grunted.

"Please!" she begged. "You can eat me. The baron never knew how many of us you captured. I can't go back!"

The giant grinned. He raised his club and then stopped and scowled, suddenly suspicious. "Where's the boy?"

I stepped forward, the rope safely tucked out of sight in the corner of our cell. "Leira," I said, "stop it. What are you doing?"

"I give up."

"No!"

"Quiet!" bellowed the giant, pointing his club at me. "Let her talk!"

"Kill me," she urged.

"What are you doing?!" I repeated.

"I said *quiet!*" the giant roared and before I could get out of the way, he swung his club at me.

I threw up my right arm for protection, but the metal spikes found their mark, slicing easily through the meat of my arm. The force of the blow sent me crashing into the wall. Pain sailed up my arm and squeezed my throat shut.

The giant pulled the club loose, then grinned and leaned close to Leira. "And now for you."

Don't let him hurt her!

I struggled to my feet to stop him from hurting Leira, but I was too slow. He raised the club high—

No!

But then, even from inside the dungeon, I heard the rattle of carriage wheels and the whinny of horses outside the window.

The baron.

Maul stopped in mid-swing, looked at the narrow window, looked back at Leira, then scowled and hurried out the door, locking it securely behind him.

Leira rushed to me. "Kadin!"

In pain, I slid back to the ground. I held one hand against the deep wounds in my arm to stop as much bleeding as I could, but the metal spikes had nearly torn it from my body. My arm hung useless by my side, bleeding profusely. My body was ripe with pain, and with every breath, I shook slightly. "The baron . . ." I gasped. "We have . . . to get . . . you out."

She shook her head and touched my forehead softly. "No, Kadin. I'll get the healing water."

"No," I argued.

But her mind was made up. She retrieved the flask of healing water from our pile of provisions.

I shook my head. "We have to save it . . ."

She unscrewed the cap of the flask. "No, Kadin. Not any more."

"Get out," I breathed. "The hairpin . . . try to . . ."

"It's impossible. We'll find another way." She leaned over me. "We have to take care of your arm."

"No time . . ." I tried to say more, but I was getting dizzy and I'm not sure I actually said anything at all. I shuddered. Closed my eyes. But she slapped my face. "Stay with me." I opened them again. She carefully eased my free hand away from my injured arm, revealing the deep, ragged puncture wounds left by the giant's club. "Oh, Kadin."

"It's not that bad."

"You're a terrible liar."

"So you've said."

She poured a little of the precious water onto my arm and laid the flask against the wall of the cave, propping it up beside a pair of leg irons. Then she caressed my wounds with her hand. I expected it to hurt, but it didn't. The tingling sensation I'd felt that day at the pool at Reyhan's inn returned.

Almost immediately, the bleeding stopped. The pain began to fade, then the skin started to close up over the wounds. I imagined the bones mending themselves as well. Leira tipped a few more drops of the water onto the most serious wounds, and it felt as if someone were gently squeezing my arm. The pressure wasn't painful, but soothing. In a matter of moments the swelling had disappeared, the discoloration was gone, and the strength in my arm began to return.

I flexed my arm and curled my fingers. "Amazing."

Leira placed a hand on my shoulder. "I was buying time before. Acting. When I told the giant to—"

"I know."

"Just so you could hide the rope."

"Yes. I know."

Outside the dungeon, I could hear Maul enthusiastically greeting the baron, explaining how he'd done all he could to keep us alive and protect us, but that one of the prisoners was damaged when he found him.

I stretched my arm to test its flexibility and when I did, I accidentally bumped the flask of healing water. It tipped over. "Oh, no!" I snatched it up before any more could drain out, but the flask was nearly empty.

"Oh, Leira," I whispered. "I'm so sorry."

"It's all right." There was a sense of finality in her words. "The important thing is that you're okay."

I saw the hope fading from her eyes. "Don't give up." We stood. "It's not too late. We're going to make it."

"Sure."

As I put my hand on her shoulder to comfort her, I noticed the spot on the ground where the water had spilled. "Leira, look."

Some of the water had poured onto the dirt floor of the cell, but some had splashed against the leg irons. Where those drops had landed, thin tendrils of smoke curled up as the metal disintegrated.

Leira knelt to inspect it more carefully. "The water is eating away at the—"

"—at the metal. Yes." An idea was forming in my mind.

Healing water. It's healing water . . .

"But how?" she said. "It's only water?"

"Remember the dragon? The water burned into its face." I picked up the flask, swished around what was left inside. "This water came from the inn, from those who serve the king!"

"But here . . ." She caught on. "This is an evil place." She could see me smiling. "Kadin, what are you thinking? Even if we were to pour this in the lock, we'd never be able to get the door open—"

"Not the door." My eyes traveled up the wall and I pointed. "The window."

CHAPTER SEVENTEEN

Poison

I retrieved the rope from the other side of the room. "If I can get up to the window, I can pour the water on the bars, and we can get out of here."

"Well done," she exclaimed. "But hurry. The baron will be down here any minute."

From this distance I doubted I could throw the boot up through the bars. Instead, I leaned the walking stick against the wall at an angle and kicked it hard. The stick broke in two, splitting where the arrowhead had been embedded into it. The arrowhead went spinning across the dirt floor. Leira reached down to pick it up.

"Careful," I warned. "They put poison on the tips of their arrowheads."

She held it gingerly.

"Here." I walked over to her and opened my pocket. She dropped the arrowhead inside and wiped her hand on her tunic.

I broke the bottom half of the stick again to get a piece of wood about as long as my forearm. Then I tied one end of the rope to the middle of it.

"I sure hope this works." I heaved the stick toward the window. It clattered off the dungeon wall. I picked it up and tried again.

From outside the window came the venomous words of the baron, seeping toward us like poison settling into the bottom of a cup, "Take me to the prisoners."

"Follow me," answered the giant.

I threw the stick up at the window again. This time, it sailed between two of the metal bars. I paused, my heart hammering in my chest, waiting to see if one of the baron's guards would notice. When there was no response, I yanked the rope, bringing the stick firmly against the bars.

"I don't believe it," Leira said. "This just might work."

The shepherd said this staff would serve you well.

I jammed the flask of healing water into my pocket and started to climb the rope. It was hard work, but my healed arm felt stronger than ever.

When I got to the window, I pulled myself up and peered cautiously outside. From what I could see, Maul had already led the baron into the castle. "We need a distraction," I called to Leira.

"But what?"

"The phoenix head. Throw me the head of the walking stick."

"Kadin, I—"

"Do it!"

She grabbed the head of the phoenix and tossed it to me. Feet against the wall, left hand wrapped around the rope, it took three tries before I caught it in my right.

I held it up to the sunlight coming through the window, trying to remember just the right positioning of the eyes to allow them to capture and refocus the sun's rays.

"From the ashes," I heard Leira whisper, "new life will arise."

Beyond the dungeon walls I heard the giant open the first door. He was at the top of the stairs.

Come on! Come on!

I twisted the carved head slightly to the left, then right again, and at last found the angle. The eyes grabbed the rays of sunlight, throwing out two beams of light that met on the ground. I tilted the stick to focus the beams on the straw beneath the baron's carriage.

At first there was only a slight curl of smoke, and I feared that Maul and Baron Dorjan would get to us before I could get the fire started, but then a thread of flame appeared, and a moment later, the entire pile of straw burst into flame, engulfing one wheel of the carriage.

From there things happened fast.

Smoke billowed toward the sky as the wooden body of the carriage caught fire. Two of the guards who'd come with the baron cried out, drawing their swords and looking around. I ducked before they could see me.

My left arm was losing strength, and I dropped the phoenix head and held onto the bars with both hands.

The shouts of the guards were just what we needed. Outside the dungeon's door, I could hear Maul jangling his keys. If he opened the door now, he would see me trying to escape and would certainly smash me against the wall, creating one more stain in his dungeon.

But before he could swing the door open, he must have heard the cries from outside. I heard Baron Dorjan curse loudly on the other side of the door, then he and Maul retreated up the stairs.

"Quick," Leira called to me. "Put the water on before they come back!"

Right hand grasping a bar, I retrieved the flask with my left and, holding the cap in my teeth, twisted it open. A few drops of water spilled to the ground.

Careful!

I wasn't sure how I would apply it to the bars; I hadn't really thought about that part. Splashing it toward them would waste too much water. I'd planned to pour it into one hand and apply it with the other, but hadn't remembered I would need to keep holding on somehow.

"Hurry, Kadin!" cried Leira.

Outside, guards were hurling buckets of water at the carriage, and Baron Dorjan was screaming at the giant, blaming him for the fire and demanding that the prisoners be brought to him *immediately.*

Maul disappeared into the castle again.

Oh no.

This was our last chance.

In a moment of desperation I tipped the flask into my mouth.

"What are you doing?" Leira shouted.

If the bars holding the stick are eaten away, the rope will fall and take you with it!

I held the ledge rather than the bars, just in case. Once I had a mouthful of the healing water, I sprayed it at the metal bars on the side of the window opposite the rope.

"Kadin, he's coming!"

I tried again, using the last of the water.

This time the bars crumbled in a shower of steaming metal shards. Thankfully, the ones holding up the rope hadn't been hit by the water and stayed secure.

With one hand I broke the last remnants of the smoking bars, and then wrestled myself up through the window. "Come on, Leira! Hurry!" I called. Once free, I dropped the ten feet or so to the ground outside the castle. The guards were preoccupied with the fire, and none had turned my way. "Leira! Climb up!"

She scrambled up the rope and tipped out the window next to me, just as the dungeon door burst open and Maul arrived. The sound of his enraged cry when he discovered the empty dungeon made the hair on the back of my neck stand up. Leira and I ran around the corner of the castle in the opposite direction from the burning carriage.

"We made it," I breathed.

But Leira gasped.

Standing before us, holding a dagger, was Baron Dorjan himself.

◆ ◆ ◆ ◆

"Hello." His voice was soothing, mesmerizing. He peered down at us from his height of nearly seven feet tall. The baron's face was stunningly handsome, not at all like I'd imagined it would be. He wore a black leather coat that swept behind him in the breeze and fluttered like the wings of a giant bat. "Guards," he shouted, and before we could even turn around, four of his men had gathered around us with their swords drawn.

Baron Dorjan narrowed his eyes at me, then looked at Leira. "Mmm . . . My dear. I have special plans for you."

I stepped in front of her. "No."

"I'm not afraid of you!" Leira yelled defiantly at the baron.

"Then I guess I'll have my work cut out for me. It'll be even more fun than the last time." He turned to the giant, who had huffed up the stairs and was lumbering toward us with clenched fists. "Maul, I thought you told me the prisoners were locked up?"

"They were." His voice was like thunder.

"And yet, here they are. And my carriage lies in ashes as well?"

The giant was silent, but he glared at me and Leira.

"Well then." In one fluid motion the baron cocked his arm back, and deftly hurled his dagger at Maul's neck. The blade sank to the hilt into the thick neck of the surprised giant. It seemed comical to me that the baron would even think that a tiny weapon like that could hurt a giant Maul's size.

Maul grunted, scratched once at the dagger, and then let out a low growl. He raised his club to smash all of us, but before he could bring it down, his face reddened and his breathing became choked.

The dagger must have been dipped in poison.

The same as the archers use on their arrowheads!

I slid my hand into my pocket.

Baron Dorjan calmly tilted his head to watch the giant die, and when he spoke, he seemed to read my mind: "My own recipe, with a little help from my collection of Baskian vipers."

The giant clutched his throat and collapsed to his knees, sending a huge tremor through the ground. Then he fell forward and lay still.

"It looks like I'll have to get a new giant," the baron said. He faced Leira and me again, reached into his cloak, and pulled out two parchments.

"Our pardons," Leira whispered.

"Maul was kind enough to retrieve these from your packs."

With a sudden burst of blue flame, a ball of fire appeared in the baron's hand. Before I could move, the fiery sphere had engulfed the pardons. In a matter of seconds they were consumed.

"No!" I cried. Without those pardons we would never be allowed into the city of Celestia. The ashes of our pardons fell between the baron's fingers and were carried away by the breeze. He brushed off his hands. "What a shame." He was eyeing the other side of the river where the city of Celestia lie. "To come this close and then fail."

By then the rest of the guards had given up trying to salvage the carriage and had gathered behind us. I felt enraged but also helpless. To our left was the giant's castle, in front of us stood the baron, and Maul's body blocked the right. We were trapped. Less than a hundred feet past the baron was a cliff, and somewhere far below that flowed the dark river. Beyond the river lay the land of the ancient kings. The baron saw me staring in that direction.

"You want to have a look?" He produced a spyglass from his pocket. "Here," he said, walking toward Leira. "Ladies first."

The guards hadn't grabbed me yet. That was good.

I noticed Leira's hands trembling. I wanted to move, but held back. Our only chance was if the baron came close to me.

Dorjan placed his hands atop Leira's. "Let me help you." He steadied the telescope for her, directed it toward the city that lay beyond the dark river. It looked like she was trying to pull away, but he was too strong for her, and he held her fast: "See how beautiful it is?" The way he held the telescope, sunlight glinted off a ring he wore on his right hand.

And suddenly, it all came together. "You used to live there," I said.

He lowered the spyglass and studied me for a moment. "Long ago. But I left. It's not all that people say."

"No," Leira countered. "You were banished. You're the knight."

"No," I said. "He's the vizier."

The baron looked at me quizzically.

"Your signet ring." I gestured toward him. "You were second-in-command. You were the one who gave the poison to the knight when he tried to kill the king."

A smiled snaked across his face.

"What happened to the knight?" I asked. "Did you kill him?"

"Buried alive," he said through his grim smile, "in the hills of the western plains. I did it myself."

I remembered the first time I ever read the Book of Blood, remembered the evil it spoke of, imprisoned in the hills. It said that one day it would be released. "He's not dead," I said. "He's going to return, and he won't be too happy with you."

The baron's lips tightened. "One last chance, now." He offered me the spyglass. "Take a peek at the land you'll never visit?"

Though it repulsed me to even let him near me, if we were going to get away I had to. "Yes. All right."

He strode toward me, and I reached for the telescope as the guards began laughing behind me. I looked at Leira. "Soon it'll all be over," I said. "Soon."

She looked at me curiously.

"Soon," I repeated.

"Soon," she said, remembering Alcion's words.

I accepted the spyglass with my left hand and drawing my right hand out of my pocket, swiped the edge of the razor-sharp arrowhead against the back of the baron's wrist.

He gasped and jerked backward. For a moment he stared at the cut, more in shock than in pain. But he knew what kind of poison the arrowhead had been dipped in. He knew the pain would come. He hesitated for just a moment, but one moment was all we needed.

"Get them!" he screamed to the guards.

But it was too late. In the stunned instant when he'd pulled his hand back, I had rushed toward Leira and taken her hand in mine. Together we bolted toward the edge of the cliff before any of the guards could react.

Behind me I could hear the strangled cries of Baron Dorjan as the poison that he himself had designed began to work on him. "Stop them," he coughed to his men.

Leira and I were less than fifty feet from the edge of the cliff now. Behind us, the sound of footsteps grew louder. I ventured a glance back and saw the guards in close pursuit.

"Kadin—" Leira said. We were twenty feet from the lip of the escarpment. "—do you know what you're doing!"

Maybe, maybe—

"Yes!"

The only way to pass into the city is to cross the river.

But no one lives who tries to—

Ten feet.

"Stop them!" The baron's voice was choked with rage and pain. It was weaker now and would only get weaker.

Five.

And then—

"Jump!" I yelled.

Hand in hand, Leira and I leapt from the edge of the cliff and launched ourselves into space.

For a moment it almost seemed like we hovered in midair, and then, with dizzying speed, we plummeted toward the dark river curling and churning more than two hundred feet below us.

I felt Leira pull away from me, and the fall seemed to last forever. As the water rushed toward us, I wondered if it were even possible to survive a fall from such a height. I doubted it.

The water swirled below me, coursing past unseen rocks. *You'll land on a rock and it'll all be over.*

You'll—

But I didn't land on a rock. Instead I crashed into a pocket of foam between two boulders. Before I could sink low enough for the debris at the bottom of the river to trap my feet, the current swept me downstream.

I splashed to the surface and tried to call out Leira's name, but when I opened my mouth I swallowed a mouthful of dark water instead. The river sucked me under.

Swimming hard, I made it to the surface again. "Leira!"

Somewhere just on the other side of the shore rose the walls of the legendary city of Celestia, but every time I tried to swim toward it, the current tugged me under again. Light and darkness devoured each other as I battled the water and gasped for breath, trying to find footing, trying to get to the riverbank.

Then I saw Leira ahead of me, floating facedown in the water.

"No!"

I struggled to swim toward her, but the pressure of the water overwhelmed me and the force of the current pulled me downward. Downward.

Downward.

Please, no!

I reemerged only to see the river rushing toward a narrow chute between two enormous rocks. Leira's body disappeared beneath the rapids. The entire river flowed through the tight channel so there'd be no way to stay above the surface. I tried to grab one last gulp of air but went under before I could. For a moment I struggled against the current, then everything was swallowed in a swirl of all-consuming darkness.

CHAPTER EIGHTEEN

Awakening

I remember seeing Leira's body getting pulled under and then watching the world disappear into the soul of the cold black water.

Vaguely, I recall images from my journey passing before my eyes, intermingling, flashing for a moment and then curling back again—scenes of blizzards and caves, wolves and ravens, thorns and mountains, campfires and waterfalls, bleeding trees and poisoned arrows, giants and dragons. The awful post on which my friend, Alcion, had died; my first glimpse of Leira—and my last.

All the images materialized and then faded, winding between each other, forming a pattern, then unraveling into chaos again.

Everyone has to let go of something before crossing the river, my mind told me, reciting words I'd read in the Book of Blood.

It was then that I knew I was dead.

I had to be.

The river had swallowed me and I had drowned and now I was gone and all that I had journeyed for was lost.

◆ ◆ ◆ ◆

Somewhere in the distance I could hear someone calling my name, softly, as in a dream, "Kadin . . . Kadin . . ."

I wondered for a moment how I could hear anyone speaking if I were dead, and then I wondered how I could even wonder about it if I were dead.

"Kadin."

Light seemed to wash over me, cleansing me, awakening me, coming from the voice, from everywhere.

"Wake up, Kadin. Open your eyes."

It felt like the light was filling both my mind and my soul with its very presence. Finally I coughed, opened my eyes, and saw a man leaning over me. At first his face was blurred and unrecognizable, but then as I blinked my eyes again, I could see him clearly. "Alcion?"

His face looked the same as always, yet changed in ways I couldn't even begin to describe. If you've ever seen a picture of someone and then met him in person, you understand the difference of going from two dimensions to three. That's what it was like for me—only now it was like going from three to four. Or five. Or more. I recognized everything about him, but he had a depth and reality I'd never imagined could even exist.

"You're alive?" I murmured. I propped myself up on my elbow and stared at him. "But how?" Having someone who'd been burned alive wake you up can be a little disconcerting. "Are you . . . did I die?"

"Not in the way you're thinking of," Alcion said. He took my hand and helped me to my feet. "Kadin, you have a lot to learn about this land."

I looked around. Behind me I could see the dark river. Through its spray I could barely make out the outline of the land I'd just come from. But it was fuzzy, like a dream receding into your mind as you shake loose the unconscious. I couldn't be sure if any of it were real. On this side of the river, the mists were parting, revealing a pathway to the gates of Celestia.

But Alcion didn't lead me to the city. Instead, he pointed to a motionless form lying beside the river.

"No!" I ran to Leira's side, rolled her over onto her back and brushed the wet hair from her face. Her skin felt cool and clay-like rather than warm and alive.

Please, not her!

"Alcion, you can do something, can't you? I know you can! Let her live. Please let her live. Will you ask the king? Ask him to take me instead!"

Alcion shook his head. "I'm sorry, Kadin. It doesn't work like that."

Overcome with grief I slid my arm beneath her shoulders.

She lay still.

"Leira, please. Open your eyes."

Nothing.

At different times throughout my journey I'd begged for help, cried out silent prayers, and never really considered who I was talking to. But now I did. Now I knew his name. He was the king of this land, and if he couldn't help me no one could. *King Kiral, please. Let her live. She's been searching for you her whole life. Don't let it end like this!*

But still she didn't move.

I opened my eyes and held her, hugged her wet, motionless body against my own. For a moment nothing happened, and I feared even King Kiral wasn't powerful enough to help her.

Then suddenly she shivered.

"Leira!" I cried. She coughed, and I turned her to her side so she could spit out the dark water. She did, gasped for breath, and her eyes blinked open.

"It's me," I said.

"Prince . . . ? My prince?"

"No, just Kadin."

She looked at me carefully. "But it is you. You're the one from my dream."

"No, Leira, it's Kadin."

"Kadin . . . you're—you've changed. You look just like him. You could be his brother."

She shut her eyes again, and, no longer cold and dead but warm and alive, she drew me close.

◆ ◆ ◆ ◆

After a few minutes I heard Alcion clear his throat. "It's time we get going."

Leira and I left the riverbank and followed him to the gates of Celestia.

The huge doors were guarded by two giants who were the

size of Maul, but these giants were noble and stately, not ugly and wretched.

A gentle breeze blew toward us carrying a familiar fragrance.

"Lilies," I whispered.

Alcion nodded. "It's always spring on this side of the river."

I remembered the days at the start of my journey when the land had seemed brighter, the air cleaner, the day clearer than those in Abaddon. But now, compared to what I saw stretching before me, even the towering forests in the foothills seemed dull and lifeless.

The music of Wyckell is a dry and tired tune.

The castle where the sisters live is a mere mud hut.

These were my thoughts as I saw the walls of Celestia rise before me. They glistened and danced in the sunlight. I could only wonder what kind of marvels lay inside the city.

"It's incredible," I said.

"It's home." Alcion gestured to the giants, and they swung open the mighty doors.

◆ ◆ ◆ ◆

I could try to describe that city to you, but I would fail. The world's best poets would have stared speechless at what I saw. No matter how many years I might work to get the description right, you would still think of that place in human terms and words and images. But it was so much more. An entirely new level of reality was unfolding before me. Everything I thought I knew about beauty was being rewritten before my eyes.

But before Leira and I could explore the wonders of Celestia, Alcion led us to a palace door. "You don't need me anymore," he said. "Go on. He's been expecting you."

Two nobly dressed women ushered us into the throne room where King Kiral sat on a high throne surrounded by twelve giants. Though the king was the height of a man, he seemed more imposing than the giants flanking his sides. Flying throughout the room were the white figures I'd seen pictured in Apollyon's cave and noticed flitting above the pit. At the time I'd thought they were either faeries or angels, but then I'd only caught glimpses of them. Here, they were visible in all their intricate, glorious, shining selves, and I could see that neither the term *faery* nor the title of *angel* did them justice.

Leira and I bowed low before King Kiral.

"Arise." His voice was somehow both gentle and threatening. As we stood he spoke to me first. "I always knew you'd make it, Kadin."

I struggled for what to say. "Your Majesty, I . . ."

"It's been a long journey."

"Yes."

He addressed Leira: "Welcome, daughter. Do you have your invitation?"

Fear shrouded her face. "No, Your Majesty. The baron took it from me when he imprisoned me."

"So." King Kiral looked from Leira to me. "Do you have your pardons, then?"

My heart sank. "The baron destroyed them," I said softly. "But it's my fault. Don't hold it against Leira. Please."

The king stared at us. I couldn't decipher his expression, but a chill ran down my spine as he spoke. "So you have nothing to prove that you've been invited, or pardoned, or that you've sought my kingdom at all?"

We shook our heads in stunned silence.

It's over. You won't be admitted into—

Suddenly I remembered something. "Your Majesty, Leira's name! It's in the Book of Blood. She belongs here. That proves it."

He picked up a Book of Blood that lay on a small table beside his throne. He flipped through its pages until at last he paused, trailed his finger down the paper, although I imagined he already knew the name was there. At last he nodded. "Yes," he said. "Yes, here it is. So, Leira, welcome home."

"Kadin is welcome too, isn't he?" she cried. "Oh, please,

Your Majesty!"

Since the beginning of the journey I'd been told that you must never appear before the king without a pardon. I wondered what he would do to me—I thought maybe order my execution or at least my expulsion from the city. In submission to him, I lowered my eyes and stared at the ground.

"Kadin," he said. "Look at me."

Fearing my punishment, I did as he said.

"I don't need a piece of paper to tell me who my subjects are or whom I have or haven't pardoned. I need only see their eyes."

But then why the pardons? Why—?

He was watching me, his gentle, yet terrible eyes seeing all. I trembled to look at him—this king whom time could not touch and rebellions could not topple and death could not seem to find.

"You may not have the paper that tells of your pardon, but you do have the story that tells of your journey. Your trials, your struggles, your belief in this land." The king paused and then said at last, "That's enough. Welcome home, Kadin."

I found myself speechless but finally gathered enough courage to admit something to him. "Your majesty, at the inn when Reyhan gave us our pardons, she told us that they would pardon us for crimes we would commit on the journey. I told her we didn't intend to commit any, but yet we did fail you. Both Leira and I did."

A long silence. He folded his hands on his lap. "Remember how your walking stick fell when the archer waited for you?"

"Yes."

"It was part of the journey," he said, "part of my search."

"Your search?"

"Yes."

"Are you saying you knocked over the staff?"

But how?

He nodded. "Yes, so that you could meet Leira. And when

you fought off the dogs and the archer shot at you?"

"The arrow. It missed my heart . . ." The king's ways were an unfathomable mystery to me, but I was catching on. "So that I'd be able to kill Baron Dorjan." I thought back through my trip, all the coincidences that I now realized were not coincidences at all. "A blind man, finding us in the snow . . . Maul smashing my arm and the healing water splashing against the shackles so that . . ."

"You could escape the dungeon. Yes."

As he spoke I remembered questioning Gaius about the goodness of the king in contrast to the suffering we'd experienced in our travels, and now I realized that pain is part of the journey. The King loved me enough to pursue me, even when I didn't know he was there. "It was you all along?"

"Indeed," he said, echoing the favorite word of the shepherd who'd rescued me from the swamp. There was a twinkle in the king's eye: "Indeed . . ."

What? Was King Kiral the—?

"And now." He set down the Book of Blood. "There's one more thing, isn't there?"

I was silent.

"Isn't there?" he repeated.

"Yes, Your Majesty," I said at last.

"You're wondering what is more powerful than magik."

I nodded. "Your Majesty, is it faith?"

"It is not."

"Is it love?"

"It is not. There is something greater than both faith and love. And you know what it is. Think, Kadin. Give me the answer to your own question."

I thought back to my encounters with the king's servants—Reyhan, Tobal, Gaius, Alcion, the three sisters . . . Nothing seemed to help.

I shook my head. I had no idea. I was ready to admit it to

the king, to say that I gave—

Wait . . . the three sisters . . .

Yes, the words above Michi's door.

Truth is not a tamed beast to bridle as you please.
Truth is wild and runs and pants
and leaps and climbs and breathes.

The words of Gaius: *Those who love truth will gain all.*

"It's truth," I whispered. "Truth is stronger than faith, for a person may believe in the wrong things and that will lead him astray."

"Yes. And love?"

Before I could answer, Leira, who'd been quietly listening, spoke up, "And truth is stronger than love, Your Majesty, for we may love the wrong things and it will only distract us, make us want to stay longer in Wyckell."

Truth alone, I thought, *can guide you to a love that is pure and a faith that is real.*

A smile from the king, then he held out his hands. "Now, there's a song I'd like to teach you the words to and, if I'm not mistaken, a dance that's about to begin."

Leira looked around.

I offered her my hand. "Will I do until the prince arrives?"

She smiled. "Just try not to step on my foot."

At that King Kiral laughed. And as his laughter resounded through the throne room, the musicians of Celestia began to play, and Leira and I stepped, arm in arm, into the heart of the music.

EPILOGUE

Epilogue

And so ends my dream.

And even now as I write these words, I can't help but wonder if it was really a dream after all, or perhaps, just maybe, a memory.

The stars here seem close enough to touch. I think perhaps tonight I will grab one and put it in my pocket forever.

A Note from the Author

According to some experts, *The Pilgrim's Progress* was the second-bestselling book in the world for nearly 200 years, trailing only the Bible. When John Bunyan wrote his classic allegory during his imprisonment for preaching the gospel without permission, he undoubtedly had no idea it would impact the lives of so many millions of vagabonds.

In this book I've tried to reimagine John Bunyan's tale, not through the eyes of a preacher or theologian, but through the eyes of a storyteller. Rather than offer a paraphrase of his original, I've taken the liberty of fleshing out the characters and the storyline that lie at the heart of the narrative. John Bunyan's themes and images and fragments of thought have certainly found their way into this story—but so has my own imagination, my own struggles, my own journey.

Stories live only as long as they are retold or remembered. My hope is that this retelling will help John Bunyan's epic tale live on in the hearts of a whole new generation of vagabonds.

—Steven James